THE MEN OF
BREWSTER PLACE

BY GLORIA NAYLOR

The Women of Brewster Place

Linden Hills

Mama Day

Bailey's Cafe

The
MEN
of
BREWSTER
PLACE

Gloria Naylor

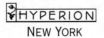
NEW YORK

Library of Congress Cataloging-in-Publication Data
Naylor, Gloria.
     The Men of Brewster Place / Gloria Naylor. — 1st ed.
        p.   cm.
     ISBN 0-7868-6421-4
     1. Afro-American men—Fiction.   I. Title.
   PS3564.A895M45   1998   97–45987
   813'.54—dc21   CIP

Designed by Christine Weathersbee

FIRST EDITION

10 9 8 7 6 5 4 3 2 1

For my father . . .
And yours

Why should it be *my* loneliness,
Why should it be *my* song,
Why should it be *my* dream
deferred
overlong?

—"Tell Me"
Langston Hughes

God slumbers in a back alley
With a gin bottle in His hand.
Come on, God, get up and fight
Like a man.

—"A Christian Country"
Langston Hughes

CONTENTS

AUTHOR'S NOTE

The author acknowledges that the character Ben died in *The Women of Brewster Place;* but she is taking poetic license to resurrect his spirit and voice to narrate major portions of this novel.

THE MEN OF
BREWSTER PLACE

DUSK

Dusk

Brewster Place became especially fond of its colored daughters as they milled like determined spirits among its decay, trying to make it a home. Nutmeg arms leaned over windowsills, gnarled ebony legs carried groceries up double flights of steps, and saffron hands strung out wet laundry on backyard lines . . .

My name is Ben. I'm a drunk. And been waiting a long time to say these next few words: This street gave birth to more than its girl children, ya know. And in all my years working as janitor on this block, I ain't seen no favoritism, one way or another, all had a hard way to go. I'm not about to argue was it harder for some than for others: Who's got it worse, the Him with nothing in his pockets, scared to turn the knob on the door; or the Her waiting on the other side to stretch that nothing—once again—for supper? When your shoes is worn down ragged and loose, what hits the ground hardest—the heel or the toe? Them are questions that ain't got no easy answer and I'm the first to admit I ain't got no fancy words. But I do know that when a She was leaning over them windowsills, calling for somebody to fetch a dollar's worth of cheese or a loaf of bread from the store, it was most likely a He who got up from the stoop or from a game of dominoes to rattle around in his pocket for the spare change to manage it. And I myself done helped many an old lady carry groceries up these rickety steps; young ones too if they was far gone pregnant or it was kinda late and I felt it just wasn't safe. Try as I might, it's hard to keep lightbulbs from getting bust up in these narrow hallways. Sometimes the younger kids'll take 'em out and smash 'em on the steps for devilment; or you'd get them older ones like C.C. Baker, hoping to work a much nastier business in the dark. You gotta watch out for the womenfolk.

Their perspiration mingled with the steam from boiling pots of smoked pork and greens, and it curled on the edges of the aroma of vinegar douches and Evening in Paris cologne that drifted through the street where they stood together—hands on hips, straight-backed, round-bellied, high-behind women who threw their heads back when they laughed and exposed strong teeth and dark gums. They cursed, badgered, worshipped, and shared their men.

But their men loved them too. And many hung in here on this street when the getting woulda been more than good because of them—and their children. There's a lot of sad things in this world; but a poor man having to keep looking into the eyes of a poor woman with no earthly reason why is one of the saddest things I know. And I saw it over and over here on Brewster Place. The Italians were the first. The street was full of 'em when I started back in the fifties. A sprinkling of Irish here and there. But they stayed mostly over in building 313 where Brother Jerome now sits playing that piano; and they were mostly old ladies who never much

left their apartments except for a sunrise Mass. Memory is a
funny thing: When I think about the folks changing on this
block, it ain't a year that comes to mind. It's the sound of
them high top shoes, with the metal hooks, stepping over
dirty water flowing down the sewer drain. The swish, swish,
of thick double petticoats under long black skirts. Not a
face, not a face in sight; just them thick shoe heels meeting
the wet cobblestone, and then just a peek of the back of their
heads. White, white hair with a tiny bit of black lace pinned
to the top. Living in the basement apartment, right next to
the wall, what else would I see? And hiding out to take a sip
or two, it being Sunday and all, what else would I hear? The
thud of those old ladies' shoes; rounding my building to take
the alley way—the quickest way—to the boulevard. And I
don't know what year it all changed, but the high-tops became patent leather with T-straps, and it was thick black
hair in braids or French knots with that same tiny bit of dark
lace pinned to the top. Another kind of Mass. Another kind
of footstep click, clicking to round my building taking the
alley way to the boulevard. Angelina. Victoria. Maria Ce-
leste. Calling to each other in the early afternoon with those
names like music. Funny, with the Italians I can remember
their men children, but not their men. The young bucks
leaning against the wall, running their hands down their
lean thighs to snag a thumb in the front pocket of them
jeans, smoking and leaving cigarette butts stuck in the cracks
of the mortar.

I'd appreciate if you wouldn't do that.

You talking to me, shit sweeper?

And I'd think to myself, Yeah, I'm sweeping up for you shits. But the older ones mostly left me alone. You see, thinking the things I really felt instead of saying them meant I was a nice colored man. And since the landlord was a post office box in another city, and their radiators leaked, or the sinks backed up, or arthritis kept them from sweeping down the front steps 'cause those teenagers sure weren't gonna do it, meant that even if I'd been an uppity colored man, nobody would much care. Three buildings on the east; three on the west; and the wall blocking light from the south. A dead end street. Full of shadows. It always feels like dusk on Brewster Place. And this job was a step up for me; I never denied that. But those young white boys had to deny, *had* to deny it was worth more than shit, 'cause they didn't even have that—and who could sleep through Brewster Place's long dark nights without hanging on to some kind of dream?

But the Italians finally did what the Irish did and what the Poles did before them—died off or faded away. Time left these buildings a little shabbier, the railings a little shakier, the sidewalks a bit more cracked and tar stained. The only things that didn't seem to change was me—and that brick wall. I was still drinking. It was still there. And this place was still a dead end street when "company came."

Brewster Place rejoiced in these multicolored "Afric" children of its old age. They worked as hard as the children of its youth, and were as passionate and different in their smells, foods, and codes from the rest of the town as the children of its middle years. They clung to the

*street with a desperate acceptance that whatever was here was bet-
ter than the starving southern climates they had fled from. Brewster Place knew that unlike its other children, the few who would
leave forever were to be the exception rather than the rule, since
they came because they had no choice and would remain for the same
reason.*

Like me, some came from sharecropping in Tennessee; others Mississippi, South Carolina. And others from just somewhere else around the city, hopping like checkers on a
board; when there's no moving up, you just move around.
But a street is a street is a street. Give me a nickel for each
time I've swept down these steps or raked garbage from the
sewer and I'll give you every paycheck I made in return. A
better bargain for me, believe it. A street is a street is a
street. It's cement and sand and water mixed up to dry. It
wears with time, gets dirt and tar ground into its surface; it
cracks and finally needs to be patched. A street is a street is
a street.

But let me tell you about men: If you put him on the likes
of a Park Avenue and he feels he has no worth, then it's not
Park Avenue. If you put him on the likes of a Chicago South
Side and he feels he has worth, then it's not the South Side.
We all live *inside*. That's the first thing I got to say. And the
second thing is to tell the *whole* story. I don't know a man
who would be anywhere without a woman. And don't know
a woman who'd be anywhere without a man. It's how God
did it; and we sure can't undo it. We can try; and probably
pass off some pretty good imitations of life. But since it

looks like we're here only once—and for a short time at that—why not go for the real deal? And here's what you're gonna always get from me: My name is Ben. I'm a drunk. And I've been working on this block close to forever. And if Brewster Place could talk, it wouldn't tell you nothing much different than what I've said: It's concrete and mortar, bricks and wood, iron railings and glass windows. And every black man, every mother's child, who found himself here hoped for better—every one. Not all of them prayed for better, 'cause some didn't believe in God. Not all of them worked for better, 'cause some of them were lazy as sin. Not all of them even really wanted better, 'cause it takes courage to live with change. But if there was a woman anywhere around him, he had to hope for better 'cause she was the other half; the other arm, the other eye—stepping right up on his shoulders to reach for a dream. And that's about as much poetry you'll ever get from the likes of me. I don't know fancy words, but I do know men. And the ones here, proud most of 'em, pitiful some—but hard working, all of 'em. If they was working at a job or just working at despair. And with each of 'em—no matter who he was—there was always a Her in his story.

BEN

Near to sixty-eight years old when I look back over my life, one of the things that bothers me the most is that I ain't never been in a situation where anybody ever called me sir. I was raised by Grandma and Grandpa Jones in a little backwater town of Tennessee. The place was so small it ain't never had a real name coming into being because of the sharecroppers who settled there to raise cotton on Percy Wall's rich bottomland. Somehow all that got mixed together to come out as the Richland Plantation. No point in looking for it on the map 'cause Richland only existed in the map of our minds. A place so poor none of us felt the difference when the Great Depression came. A place that knew backbreaking work—nine months a year—from the planting, weeding, and picking of cotton. So much cotton it touched the horizon each way you looked.

My grandparents' house was one of about forty shacks

that was clustered together on the northeast section of the land. The only businesses was the general store and post office that Percy Wall set up for us, and a juke joint and church we set up for ourselves. And that was Richland: a place where you worked until you were bone-tired and then had a choice to pray—or party—the misery away. Some did both; and in a small place we knew exactly who they were.

My grandfather didn't take to either one. The gin house ain't getting the last of my money, he would say. He could be found in the same place Saturday night or Sunday morning: sitting in his porch rocker with a closed Bible in his lap. Grandpa Jones never opened that Bible during all the time I knew him. Although he never stopped me and Grandma Jones from the services, he only went to church on Resurrection Sunday when the sinners were called to come down front and sit on the mourner's bench. It was a vengeful God that the minister always preached on that Sunday—a God of fire and brimstone—and it was a God Grandpa Jones could understand.

He was a bitter man. "I'm opening this Bible when someone shows me the place that says white people is going to hell."

It did no good for Grandma Jones to tell him that the Bible spoke for all people—black or white—redeeming themselves or damning themselves by what was in their hearts. Some hearts is blacker than others, Grandpa Jones would argue back. Some hearts need a special place in any man's Bible to be sent to a special part of hell.

My grandparents were born in slavery on the same Virginia plantation. Both of 'em still only children when freedom came. They ain't had no stories of chains or whips, families being broken apart and sold down the river, that kinda thing you see now on TV or in the movies. Grandma Jones had worked in the plantation kitchen, and was such a good cook she'd be hired out to the next plantation over when there was big parties or celebrations in the works. "There I was," she'd say, "a little bit of a thing and in a half hour I could make up enough biscuit dough to feed a hundred with one hand tied behind my back."

Grandpa Jones had worked in the stables and was in training to be a coachman. He loved horses and was glad he had a chance to take care of them. And he liked driving, especially since it gave him a chance to hear what was on the master's and mistress's mind. With the exception of the rumors about a war brewing between the states they talked most of their business freely around the slaves. As if you couldn't hear them—or care. Grandma Jones had lots of stories about the way the house servants learned to listen at doors or through windows to round out the full picture of what was really going on in the white man's world. The one story Grandpa Jones had to tell was never told to me or even Grandma Jones. It was a story that he carried inside; because there was no words he could use to talk about silence:

There are two things that happen odd that day. The sun rises a blazing red which means a storm was coming from the east but the day stays fair and clear. And Dulane, the overseer, sends Grandpa's sister, who everybody calls Sister, away from the fields with the other young children to go pick dewberries for a cobbler that he says the madam has her heart set on having for supper. But it isn't dewberry season with the fruit still green on the bush. Dulane puts Big Sam in charge of the fields that morning, saying that he has other business in town. The others watch him ride toward the woods—thinking he's gonna check on the children before he goes off in the opposite direction for the only road that could take you to town. They even look long enough to see him ride into the woods—but they never see him come out.

But they do see Sister come out of the woods, stumbling toward the fields, calling for her mother. When the child gets close enough they see the blood running down her legs. Blood soaking the back of her dress. Blood running from the corner of her mouth on the side of her face where she'd been beaten so bad her eye had swollen shut. The girl is ten years old. And the call goes out in the fields—one row to another—"Get her Mama; get May Sue." And when the woman comes running through the fields, everyone she passes stands still in silence. Mama Thorn, the midwife, helps her carry the child to their shack. They try to stop the bleeding, but she's been ripped up too much inside. And what they couldn't do in the black man's world, they try in the white one's—to save the girl from dying.

Mama Thorn binds her up as tight as she can before they carry her to the back door of the big house. The kitchen help is silent. The housemaids are silent. The butler is silent. The only cry that goes up— from floor to floor of the mansion— "Call the Missus; call the Missus." She comes, takes one look at the child, and sends for the doctor. And they send Grandpa, only twelve years old, but who has the skill to ride like the wind. He's so frightened that he forgets and rides up to the front of the doctor's house. He jumps off the horse and bangs on the front door. The black housekeeper flings the door open, asks him if he's crazy, and sends him around the back. She makes him wait as punishment for stepping out of his place. And by the time the doctor gets dressed and rides back to the big house, the girl is dead. Dulane is called into the master's study and mistress stands guard outside the door to keep the house servants from eavesdropping. Whatever goes on between him and Dulane is never spoken about as the overseer goes back to work.

They hold Sister's funeral in silence. Grandpa doesn't hear the minister as he talks about a better world waiting for Sister. About a true and loving God opening up his arms to receive those pure in heart. None of it makes any sense to him so the minister might as well have been silent. The slaves all go back to work. A new day begins. But Grandpa listens for someone to say, It was wrong. He listens in the fields, in the slave quarters beside the door of the house servants—all in vain. Even if only among themselves there is some cry of No. Even if they have to whisper, No. But they all remain silent. As if Sister didn't live or—more important—hadn't died. As if none of it had happened. And that is when he understands that— freedom or no freedom—his people are doomed. It doesn't matter what's in their hearts; what's in your heart only God hears. But they—each of them—need to hear, among themselves somewhere, somehow, that this was wrong. The Lord giveth and the Lord taketh away, the minister had said. And Grandpa had yelled out No. No, he don't. All eyes turned to him before his mother slapped him. Boy, shut your mouth, you hear? Shut your mouth. Be a man.

And so it was a silent old man who sat on his porch rocker. A man who shunned the church, holding a closed Bible, while he searched for another kind of God in another kind of world than the one who told black men that the only way to be a man was to suffer and be still. I believe that things woulda probably turned out different for me if my grandfather woulda lived longer. But him dying when I was seven meant Grandma Jones was left to raise me. And it was left to both of us to make some kinda living.

Grandma Jones could never work in the cotton fields because of the ulcers on her leg that just got worse with time. She kept them bandaged the best she could but the three rooms of our house always smelled of mustard plaster, sweat, and dried pus. I helped her to take in washing so we wouldn't be sent to the poorhouse. It was my job to cut the wood for the huge iron kettle in the front yard; then fill it with water and keep the fire going. Grandma would get around on an old wooden chair that she dragged to the front porch and then, getting out the chair, let herself down on the steps, dragging the chair behind her until she was sitting in the yard. From there she could stir the clothes boiling in that huge kettle. After she was through, it was my turn again to fill a huge tin tub with cold water for her to do the rinsing and me to hanging them up finally on the line. And that's how we made do until I was big enough to go into the fields with the rest of the workers. Be grateful for what the Lord gives you, she said over and over throughout my childhood. Be grateful. I always wondered which Lord she meant—her God or the one my grandfather waited on to wreak vengeance.

When I was seventeen she died, and I was on my own. I guess I coulda stayed on that plantation but I wanted to see something of the world. Maybe even get as far as Memphis.

For some reason I was never drafted for the Second World War that was in full swing. I thought long and hard about just signing myself up. It would mean three hots and a cot— just like jail—but I figured if they want me bad enough, they'll find me. And they never did, at least not in that little hotel where I ended up working in Memphis. This wasn't one of the good hotels where the rich stayed; it was one of those second-class places that catered mostly to gamblers and railroad workers who were laying over for a day or two.

My first job was to clean the spittoons and I kept 'em shining. If you do a job, do it right my grandmother always said. But hardly a day ever passed that I didn't get tobacco juice spit on my uniform or in my hair. It made some of 'em feel good as I was there bending over to dump the spittoons to pretend they didn't see me as they let go with a wad of tobacco. The railroad workers tipped the best but they were the hardest to please. All week bowing and scraping to the passengers, they wanted a little of that respect from us to make 'em feel like men again. The pecking order I guess; except for the black bellhops and kitchen workers, there was no one under them to take the load so they just struck out sideways.

One day Billy beat up Rayburn to an inch of his life for stepping on his shoes. There was always a crap game going in the alley behind the hotel. Men who were off from work, others who hadn't yet started, and those taking their half-hour break kept the dice game rolling for most of the day. Sometimes they'd hand around a little pint of gin; I always passed on that 'cause in those days I wasn't drinking. Billy had moved up to bellhop from cleaning the spittoons 'cause the manager said he had a "good attitude." Billy was one of those bellhops who grinned when he didn't have to, bowed lower than he had to, and was one of those who ran to get coffee or ice water even when the customer said there was no hurry. Billy always hurried to do more than he was told. And he wasn't above reporting another bellhop to the boss for slacking in his duty. The other men hated him.

But coming out of those back fields, I kinda understood. There wasn't a whole lot of work for black men like us outside of picking cotton; and some would do anything to keep from having to go back to the fields. Add to that the fact you got white gloves and a pressed red uniform with gold braid; to some men this was making it into the big time. But there's getting by and there's getting by, the other men said. Billy was a house Negro and that's all there was to it.

That day when they were shooting craps, he had a half hour before reporting to work. Billy started work with shoes that shined like a mirror. Pants so creased they could cut like a knife. And his hair brushed and gleaming from pomade and Vaseline. To everybody's joy—and they didn't care to hide it—he was just about to crap out. Rayburn had a six-dollar bet against Billy and he was on the sidelines, doing what always went down before a roll, joking and jiving. Come on, Billy boy, show me another pair of eyes, the baby is crying and mama needs a new pair of shoes. Hot damn—Billy rolled snake eyes. Rayburn reached over him to pick up his money, Thank you, my man, thank you, and accidentally stepped on the toes of Billy's shoes. You mighta thought Rayburn had spit in his face. Billy jumped up screaming, "You goddamned black ape, I'll cut your fucking throat." Rayburn said, "Hang loose, man, it was an accident, I'm sorry."

Sorry wasn't good enough for Billy. He drew his blade and it took three of us to pull him off that boy. Like the saying goes, Rayburn had been cut every place but loose. We called for the ambulance. The manager called the law. They took Billy away, and the rest of us got fired. I was close to leaving anyhow. It didn't do me proud to be dressed up like the monkey who was kept in a cage near the front desk as the hotel's good-luck charm. The same monkey Billy would pose beside—his teeth shining—for the tourists who wanted to take pictures.

My next job in the city was shoeshine boy at the railroad depot. We all called ourselves boys even though in my late twenties I was the youngest one there. I was hoping to be able to move up to being a porter one day; even to getting taken on as a redcap, which meant a lot more tips and a way to see other cities besides Memphis. The shoeshine chairs were set up in a row of twelve—ten for the white customers and two spaced a bit apart for the Negro customers. Somehow all the passengers knew this arrangement without the railroad needing to put any signs up. Shine, sir—need a shine? was the call when business was slow. The man who smiled the most and popped his rag usually got a taker. What was there about white folks that made them feel comfortable when a Negro smiled? It seemed they worried about us being angry; maybe because they felt they would be if they were in our place. But it was a job to me. At two bits a shine and tips I could clear close to six dollars in a day. And unlike the other shoeshine boys I didn't mind working the Negro chairs. There was usually a line of Negro men waiting their turn for those two seats and they tipped as well as any other customer—sometimes more. Something about seeing them lined up that way with half the white seats empty made me sad. And there were the other men calling, Shine, sir—need a shine? when there was a long line of Negro customers waiting.

I guess I woulda stayed on as a shine boy if I hadn't met Elvira. She worked in the ladies' bathroom, handing out towels and keeping the sinks and floors clean. Evil Elvira the men called her, 'cause she was known not to be easy. I appreciated her for it; a woman who respected herself. And she was always with a magazine or a book in her hands when it wasn't busy in the ladies' room. And I'd always said I wanted me a girl who could read and write. Not asking for a whole lot, is it? But coming from my time and my place, it was a big thing to catch a good woman who could do both. I imagined her standing up there at City Hall and writing her name large with a flourish at the end. Perfect penmanship. And I guess my imagining it so much over the months moved into my actually wanting it—and wanting her. But when we got to talking about marriage, she said the doctor told her she'd have to leave Memphis if she was ever gonna get rid of a dry cough she had. It made her voice deeper than normal for a woman and sometimes she coughed so hard her chest hurt. We figured that country air would be better for her. Both of us had grown up on farms, so it wasn't a big leap to go back. I was just disappointed that I had to put away my dream of riding the railroads as a redcap.

It don't take much to set yourself up as a sharecropper. It's just finding the right farm to take you on. You get the old beat-up house that was left by the family before you. The man who owns the place gives you loans of your seed and equipment; and then you're in business. A business that never lets you break even 'cause by the time you bring in your crops you're still owing for the stuff you got up front. Not to mention the folks who borrowed on time from the plantation store for their flour, meal, sugar, and other dry goods. Just a little bit in the hole, was the saying each year, we're just a little bit in the hole. Well, that hole was a mile deep for most; and you ended up farming for the sake of a place to eat and sleep. A little more than slavery but a lot less than doing well.

Having a load of children meant more hands to work the cotton but more mouths to feed as well. And those who managed with their little truck gardens, raising their own chickens or pigs, keeping a milk cow or two, and taking their own corn to the mill were able to scrape a little money from the year's end. Me and Elvira was never that lucky 'cause we had only one child. A sweet girl who was crippled from birth. She was a breech baby who got her foot broken by the midwife trying to save both her and Elvira. It never did heal right. And so she kinda cripped along, but a sweet child who'd do anything you asked her, no matter how long it took. I tried to stop Elvira from yelling at her for taking so long to get water from the pump or stove wood chopped.

"She's doing the best she can," I said. "Leave her be."

But Elvira had a wicked temper and the fury of it sometimes gave me pause. "She ain't doing the best she can, and

I'm sick of carrying the load for a half-grown woman and a no-count man. Both of you lazy as sin."

None of what she said was true, which didn't stop her from saying it—or believing it. I learned a lot of things about my wife once we moved to the country; one of them was that Elvira could make herself believe just about anything she wanted. And she believed that everything white that God put in this world was good. And everything black was to be despised. Elvira didn't even take her coffee black; "It'll just make me darker," she said. We was moving in this marriage from bad to worse, and I only stayed on because of my daughter. God knows what would happen if she and Elvira were left alone. I didn't put nothing past my wife, nothing at all. I could see her sneaking away after sending the girl on an errand into town; and there she is returning to an empty house and no way to take care of herself. So, like Elvira, I thought it was a godsend when Mr. Clyde asked us if our daughter could come and clean his house. Things went well for about two months, and then I noticed that when she came home there were tears in her eyes.

"Is everything all right, baby?"

"It's fine, Daddy Ben. Just a lot of work."

"Well, anytime you think it's too much . . ."

And she began to cry. That's when she told us everything: how Mr. Clyde had been trying to mess with her almost from the beginning, how it was hard 'cause he'd follow her around the house, whispering nasty things in her ear.

"You're lying," Elvira screeched. "You know you lying."

"And when I told him," my daughter continued, "that I

was gonna tell my daddy, all he did was laugh. He laughed. And laughed."

Mornin', Ben. Mornin', Elvira.

The red pickup truck stops in front of my yard. My daughter gets out the passenger side and begins to limp toward the house. Elvira grins into the creviced face of the white man sitting in the truck with tobacco stains in the corner of his mouth.

Mornin', Mr. Clyde. Right nice day, ain't it, sir?

I watch my daughter come through the gate with her eyes on the ground, and she slowly climbs up on the porch. She takes each step at a time, and her shoes grate against the rough boards. She finally turns her beaten eyes into my face and what is left of my soul to crush is taken care of by the bell-like voice that greets us. Mornin', Daddy Ben. Mornin', Mama.

Mornin', baby, I mumble with my jaws tight.

How's things up at the house? Elvira asks. My little girl do a good job for you yesterday?

Right fine, Elvira. Got that place clean as a skinned rat. How's y'all's crops comin'?

Just fine, Mr. Clyde, sir. We sure appreciate that extra land you done rented us. We bringin' in more than enough to break even. Yes sir, just fine.

The man laughs, showing the huge gaps between his tobacco-rotted teeth. Glad to do it. Y'all some of my best tenants. I likes keepin' my people happy. If you needs somethin', let me know.

Sure will, Mr. Clyde, sir.

Aw right, see y'all next week. Be by the regular time to pick up the gal.

She be ready, sir.

The man starts up the motor of the truck, and the tune that he whistles as he drives off remains in the air long after the dust has returned to the ground. Elvira grins and waves until the red of the truck disappears over the horizon. Then right away she drops her arm and smile and turns toward our daughter. Don't just stand there gawkin'. Get in the house—your breakfast been ready.

Yes, Mama.

When the screen door has slammed shut, Elvira snaps her head around to me.

Man, what is wrong with you? Ain't you heard Mr. Clyde talkin' to you, and you just standin' there like a hunk of stone. You better get some sense in your head 'fore I knock some in you.

I stand there with my hands in my pockets, staring at the tracks in the dirt where the truck had been. I keep balling my fists in my overalls until my nails dig into my palms.

It ain't right, Elvira. It just ain't right and you know it.

What ain't right? That that gal work and earn her keep like the rest of us? She can't go to the fields, but she can clean house, and she'll do it. I see it's better you keep your mouth shut 'cause when it's open, ain't nothing but stupidness comin' out.

She turns her head and brushes me off like she would a fly, then heads toward the door of the house.

She came to us, Elvira. She came to us a long time ago.

The woman spins around with her face twisted into an airless knot. She came to us with a bunch of lies 'bout Mr. Clyde 'cause she's too damn lazy to work. Why would a decent widow man want to mess with a little black nothin' like her? No, anything to get out of work—just like you.

Why she gotta spend the night then? Why he always make her spend the night up there alone with him?

Why should he make an extra trip just to bring her tail home when he pass this way every Saturday mornin' on the way to town? If she wasn't lame, she could walk it herself after she finish work. But the man nice enough to drop her home and you want to bad-mouth him along with that lyin' hussy.

After she came to us, you remember I borrowed Tommy Boy's wagon and went to get her that Friday night. I told ya what Mr. Clyde told me: She ain't finished yet, Ben. Just like that—she ain't finished yet. And then standin' there whistlin' while I went out the back gate.

My nails dig deeper into my palms.

So! Elvira's voice gets shrill. So it's a big house. It ain't like this shit you got us livin' in. It takes her longer to do things than most folks. You know that, so why stand there carryin' on like it mean more than that?

She ain't finished yet, Ben. If I was half a man I woulda—

Elvira comes across the porch and sneers into my face. If you was half a man, you coulda given me more babies and we woulda had some help workin' this land instead of a half-grown woman we gotta carry the load for. And if you was even a quarter of a man, we wouldn't be a bunch of miserable sharecroppers on someone else's land—but we is, Ben. And I'll be damned if I'll see the little bit we got taken away 'cause you believe that gal's low-down lies. So when Mister Clyde come by here, you speak—hear me? And you act as grateful as your pitiful ass should be for the favors he done us.

I feel a slight dampness in my hands because my fingernails have broken through the skin of my palms and the blood is seeping down my fingers. I look at Elvira's dark, braided head and wonder why I don't just take my hands out of my pockets and stop the bleeding by pressing them around it. Just lock my elbows on her shoulders and place one hand on each side of her temples and then in toward each other until the blood stops. My big calloused hands on the bones of her skull, pressing in and in, like you would with a piece of dark cloth to cover the wounds on your body and clot the blood. Or I could simply go into the house and take my shotgun and press my palms around the trigger and handle, emptying the shells into her sagging breasts just long enough—just pressing hard enough—to stop my palms from bleeding.

But the grain of truth in her words is heavy enough to weigh my hands down in my pockets and keep my feet nailed to the wooden planks in the porch, and the wounds heal over by themselves. I discover that if I sit up drinking all night Friday, I can stand on the porch Saturday morning and smile at the man who whistles as he drops my lame daughter home. And I can look into her beaten eyes and convince myself that she has lied.

*The girl disappears one day, leaving behind a note saying that
she loves us very much, but she knows that she has been a burden
and she understands why we made her keep working at Mr. Clyde's
house. But she feels that if she has to earn her keep that way, she
might as well go to Memphis where the money is better.*

*Elvira runs and brags to the neighbors that our daughter is now
working in a rich house in Memphis. And she was making out awful
well because she always sends plenty of money home. I stare at the envelope with no return address, and find that if I drink enough every
time a letter comes, I can silence the bell-like voice that comes chiming
out of the open envelope—Mornin' Daddy Ben, Mornin' Daddy Ben,
Mornin' . . . And then if I drink enough every day, I can bear the
touch of Elvira's body in the bed beside me at night and not have my
sleep stolen by the picture of her lying there with her head caved in or
her chest ripped apart by shotgun shells.*

Elvira did me the great favor of running off and leaving me for another man who worked on the next plantation over. And I left Tennessee and moved up north, taking
one odd job after another, until I stumbled upon Brewster
Place; I've been here ever since. Some would say it's not
much of a job, and God knows that this street, hidden away
from the rest of the town, is not much of a place to live.
But it holds the hopes and dreams of many who find themselves here with the broken stoop railings, the grimy sidewalks, the crumbling bricks in the wall. Walking past an

open window is to smell the fried chicken, the pots of soup, the hope that rides on putting a little bit of something on the table for dinner, because this is, after all, home. Nobody knows my true story—and never will—as it is my turn to be the silent old man as I inherit more than my share of the pain riding on the question, What does it mean to be a man? Even now at sixty-eight I'm still wondering. If I had killed Clyde Haggard, the law kills me. If I had killed Elvira, the law puts me in jail for life. If I killed myself, there was no one but an understanding God to face. So I settled on killing myself—slowly with booze— and on God understanding that I'm fighting for my manhood. There is no way to face my daughter's eyes, even in memory, as she said, He laughed, Daddy. He laughed. And laughed.

So what does it mean to be a man? Sometimes when I'm sweeping outside of Brother Jerome's door and he's in there playing the blues, I think I know. But then I carry that blues with me back to my basement apartment to look around and see not an apartment really; just one large room with a lightbulb hanging from the ceiling, a bed, a few cabinets, and a hot plate with grease collecting on the edges. And when getting down to the last of my wine is to find myself scraping around for a few pennies to get another bottle, I pray I've finally found the answer to what it means to be a man, 'cause I'm doing the best I can with what I've got left.

BROTHER JEROME

He sits in the dim light waiting for the music to begin. It is morning but the day is cloudy; and on Brewster Place that is starved for light on the best of days it is gray and dark. But there is enough light to edge the borders of his mind, the island where he lives alone with music. He places his hands on the keys and begins to play: an old upright spinet with two missing keys and badly in need of a tuning. But Jerome isn't hearing the sound of the piano, he is listening for the light. Listening for the sun's rays to slant across the windowsill; enough to form a shadow, however faint, from the leaves of his mother's dying philodendron. If the light remains low, he will play the blues: slow, down-home and gritty. If the sun breaks from behind the clouds, he will still play the blues: but New Orleans-style— fast and free.

Jerome was a child that always amazed me. From the time he was five years old, legs dangling off the piano bench, he was able to make that old piano sound like it belonged off in Carnegie Hall somewhere. At first while sweeping up outside Mildred's door, I thought it was the radio playing until I went in one day to fix a broken faucet and saw it was that child at the piano. And as he grew older, his feet touching the floor, his arms able to get from one end of the keyboard to another, his hands just got better and better while his mind stayed at three years old. At seventeen he couldn't write his own name; couldn't count money or go to the store by himself; but he could make that piano tell any story that he wanted. And it was *your* story if you listened real hard. Some folks would just hear what he was playing and be amazed; while others really listened and began to cry. Because it was the blues, nothing but the blues coming from that boy's heart through that piano reading your life—and sometimes his.

> *Hot time mama*
> *Hot as she can be*
> *Hot time mama*
> *Hot as she can be*
> *Lord, she's sweet*
> *But too hot for me.*

> *Hot time mama*
> *How hot can she be?*
> *Hot time mama*
> *How hot can she be?*
> *Got a cake baking on one thigh*
> *And a pie on the other knee.*

> *Hot time mama*
> *How hot can she be?*
> *Hot time mama*

How hot can she be?
Stepped into the ocean
And boiled away the sea
Lord, that woman's sweet
But she's too hot for me.

It was hard to say that Mildred didn't love her only child; she loved him as much as she did anything else: with a lot of attention at one moment and none at the other. She'd spend a good hour cleaning the leaves of her one plant, repotting or fertilizing only to later allow it to get full of cigarette ashes and butts from her latest party. She'd yell out, "Watch my plants, y'all," only to forget about it as the party progressed. Mildred wanted life to be straight and simple: working at the dry cleaners Monday through Friday and parties on the weekend: with lots of people, laughing and fun. But God dealt her a hand that left her alone with a retarded child. Mildred took it real personal; decided it was her punishment for not going to church or refusing to marry the boy's daddy and said, "The hell with it." The damage was done so she might as well party even harder. She struggled along with him until he was five and it was getting to be too much: he was hard to feed, hard to potty-train, and finding the right school was near impossible. The Board of Education wanted her to put him away at one of those sleep-in schools and when Mildred went to visit the place she was taken back by the smells of dried urine and she found some of the children dirty and rocking back and forth in corners; and found the others just downright unhappy. Her son might be retarded but he deserved better than this. So the idea hit her to keep him out of school altogether. Didn't the doctors say that he'd never grow beyond three years old so why punish him and send him to a place like this?

Yet with him going on five and still in diapers Mildred was starting to weaken; she might not want him in that one school she'd seen but if they offered her another, she'd send him. She made sure not to visit this next school so her conscience could be clear. And using any excuse she could find to throw a party, Mildred prepared a big blowout for Jerome. It was the usual crowd that she always invited to her house parties; but she told herself this one was for the child.

Jerome got saved from the institution because Bob got drunk. Bob always got drunk when he went to parties; for him that's what a good time meant. T.J., a bluesman from way back, was on the piano, doing a decent job of some down-home boogie-woogie. Bob told the piano player to get off the bench and stop embarrassing himself. T.J. told Bob if he could do any better then try. Bob said he could do a hell of a lot better and sat down on the piano keys. He was moving up and down the keyboard playing it with his butt. The piano player tried to pull Bob off the keys. Bob fought back, and grabbing a lamp he started swinging. He was too drunk to focus on T.J. and kept missing. Everybody was laughing along with Bob who kept swinging and the piano player who kept dodging. Man, this was turning out to be one of Mildred's best parties.

The light from the lamp kept swirling and swirling

around the room, sending a hundred shadows racing from floor to ceiling, and ceiling to floor. The light moved across the radio that was turned on so people could keep dancing; moved across the faces of the drinkers, the lovers molded together on the couch—and it moved across the face of Jerome. He was sitting in a corner, licking the melted ice cream running down his arm from the cone she'd given him while placing him there in "the seat of honor," since this was supposedly his going-away party. The light and shadows kept swirling and swirling. People were getting tired of this joke and started trying in earnest to get Bob to put the lamp down; so no one noticed when Jerome got up from the chair and went to the piano. At first some thought it was the radio while others closer to the piano realized it was Jerome, all five years old of him, bent toward the keys and sending out a boogie-woogie that could have put even the likes of Jelly Roll Morton or Count Basie to shame.

Slowly the party got quiet and then it got deathly still. All eyes turned to the miracle that was happening on Mildred's old upright. Bob put the lamp down and, when the lights stopped swirling, so did Jerome's playing. They treated the child as if he was the Second Coming, urging him on to do it again. The more superstitious of them put their drinks down and headed for the door. It was Bob who figured out that the boy needed the light. Almost sober now, he picked up the lamp and swung it gently so it crossed the child's face. "Come on, Brother Jerome," he said. "Do your thing." And there it was again: his tiny left hand holding the tempo while his right sped up and down the keys. If they were church people, they would have prayed. But they were party people and so they partied; all night with Bob swinging the light and Brother Jerome, his hands sticky from ice cream, at the keyboard.

A hundred wild horses couldn't separate Jerome from Mildred after that night. Her being the mother of a special child meant that, somehow, she was special as well. Didn't she give birth to the boy? A genius. That's what all her friends were calling him as he played for each of her parties. An out-and-out genius. Mildred started charging admission to her house parties that were now in great demand. With what she earned from Jerome playing and her job at the dry cleaners, she was able to afford a new TV and living-room set.

They soon discovered that Brother Jerome didn't need a swinging lamp to set him off—any kind of light would do, especially sunlight. So the sun, of all things, became Mildred's baby-sitter. She would sit Jerome at the piano, make sure the window shades were pulled up, and leave for work. He never moved as the sunlight came through the windows bringing him the blues. If he got hungry, he used his left hand to pick up the bologna sandwich and jar of strawberry Kool-Aid she'd left, while his right hand kept the melody going. Sometimes the vibrations from the keyboard would cause the Kool-Aid to spill on his sandwich, making the bread soggy, but he ate it anyway. And if he had to go to the bathroom, he went in his diapers. Jerome wasn't potty trained until he was nearly seven years old. And even then, sometimes, he'd wet himself at the piano if me or his cousin Hazel didn't drop by to check on him. Hazel would pull the shades so it was easier to get him to stand up and go to the bathroom. But sometimes he would play the whole day through as long as there was light from those two dusty living-room windows. Twelve years later and he was still playing. Now a chubby teenager, his soft body bent over the keys, his ginger-colored skin moist from sweat, he played until his fingers were sore.

His music was telling us about our lives and he didn't even know it. Or maybe in the smallest part of his small brain he did. Maybe he heard the Amens coming from a tired man dragging his body up the cracked and dirty stoop of 314 from a job where he was overworked and underpaid. The Amens from an apartment in 312 where a man is fighting back tears as he smashes his fist into a wall to keep from hitting the bitter woman who's thrown his life back into his face telling him that whatever he's doing is not enough. The Amens from 316 as a man turns over in bed having lost the strength to get up and keep looking for another low-paying job. The Amen brothers coming from every brick; every piece of concrete and iron railing on Brewster Place as Jerome played, filling the street with the sound of a black man's blues. . . .

BASIL

Winter's the only season I don't sit out and watch the sunrise. And it's the only season I'm glad for this dark basement apartment that stays nice and warm being right next to the furnace room. Although it's no guarantee we're gonna get through the winter with these furnaces working proper. One or more of 'em is sure to break down before spring comes and then do I catch hell. Not that I can blame folks; it's bad enough you gotta live on a street like this without freezing yourself to boot. And keeping the kitchen stove heated up and the oven door open means a gas bill too large for most to pay.

But so far so good this year and it's been a cold winter. A week hasn't gone by without some snow falling and a couple of 'em have been big storms. But the snow never stays white on Brewster Place. It can look like a fairyland the first night as it falls; then come the morning and it's already speckled with grime and smoke from these old furnaces. Add to that the people slushing through it and the exhaust from cars and it's a gray mess of ice and water. But I can't remember a winter worse than this one except the time that Mattie Michael moved in. It seemed that half of the moving van was full of nothing but plants. All kinds big and small. And it made me sad to think she'd have to watch most of 'em die.

She was moving into the building closest to the wall and there's no sunlight in apartment 2E. The wall reaches up high enough to block whatever little light might try to come that way. I took it upon myself to warn her about that. "Ma'am, most of them plants ain't gonna make it up there in 2E." And she told me something that shows the kind of woman she was. "Them that live, live. And them *that die, die." And that's Mattie Michael. No self-pity. Just take life and wrestle with whatever it gives you. Rumor had it that it had given her a no-good son who caused her to be on Brewster Place; but Mattie never had nothing to say on that subject and so far as I'm concerned it wasn't that at all. One of the finest women I know. Always ready to give a helping hand—and a good dose of advice—to anybody who asked. The only thing I did know—for a fact—is that she ended up on Brewster Place, just like the rest, 'cause she had no choice. And she stayed for the same reason.*

I stood at my mother's grave site and prayed for snow. I wanted to bring back the last day when she was truly happy.

When we left the precinct, the wide soft flakes were floating in gentle layers on the November air. I reached out and tried to grab one to give her, and laughed as it melted in my hand.

Remember how I used to cry when I tried to bring you a snowflake and it always disappeared? I held my face up to the sky and let the snow fall on my closed lids.

Oh, God, Mama, isn't it beautiful?

Beautiful? You always hated the snow.

Not now, it's wonderful. It's out here and free, like I am. I love it! And I love you, Mama. I put my arm around her shoulder and squeezed. Thank you.

Yes, I thank my mother. I thank her for putting up her house for bail. For believing in me. And I thank her for not using whatever little money she had left, running me down to blow my brains out, when I caused her to lose it all. There she was, forced to leave her beautiful home to live on a street like Brewster Place. And you know what the funny thing is? I used those three years, when I didn't have the courage to call or write, doing exactly what I promised myself: I'm gonna pay her back.

I worked two full-time jobs and a part-time on Sunday until I had enough money. I was starting to feel like the man I always wanted to be. There I was, for three years, saving two checks each week from the umbrella factory and United Canning Goods while living at the YMCA on my part-time job, flipping hamburgers. Three years. I never missed a pay-check for my savings. I would lie in a room no larger than a prison cell and imagine what it was going to be like when I brought her the money.

Snapshot: My walking up the steps to her apartment with the money in my wallet. Her opening the door and crushing me in her arms. I knew you'd come back, baby.

Snapshot: My standing out on the street and calling up to her window, waving the check in my hands. Open the door, Mama. Open the door.

Snapshot: I pull up into Brewster Place with a moving van and her racing down those rickety steps to meet me.

For each day I was away from her, I had a daydream of what it would be like when I returned to honor her trust in me. To take her away from that dead-end street where her love had placed her. One day when I was halfway to my goal, I just had an urge to see the street where she lived. I was too much of a coward to go during daylight because she might spot me and I wasn't ready for that. This visit was just a dress rehearsal for the day I felt I would truly become a man.

It was an early evening in the first part of winter. And it was everything I had imagined and worse. The buildings looked as if they were one good season away from becoming condemned. The cracked sidewalks, the leaning stoop railings, the crumbling bricks on the base of the buildings. The smell of cabbage and day-old grease lingering in the air. An old man with stooped shoulders was bundling newspapers to be set out with the morning trash.

"You looking for someone?" he asked.

My heart was beating so fast I could hardly hear him. "No," I said, "just looking."

"Well, we ain't got no more vacancies, and won't be none for a while. Maybe come spring."

"You're the super here?" I asked.

"Yeah. Just call me Ben. I can take your name in case something unexpected comes around soon."

"No, I can't do that." I said it so sharply, he gave me a puzzled look and this time he really focused in on my face. Why was I acting so guilty? You'd think I had committed a crime. But then again, maybe I had.

"I mean," I continued, "there's no need, I've found a place a few blocks over that I'll probably take. Well, I'll see ya."

I left trying not to give into an urge to run. Then he'd really remember me. And he'd tell her all about me. Which was nothing but fear talking, irrational fear. This man wouldn't even remember me by the morning. Or I hoped that he wouldn't.

And with it finally in place, all forty-seven thousand dollars, enough for a down payment with monthly payments I could meet, I went to Brewster Place once again to find her gone. Next address: Pine Acres Cemetery. I put the check at the bottom of her tombstone: Mattie Michael; and I saw the last three years of my life taken by the wind and sent flying up among the branches of the tall pine trees.

So where to from her grave? I couldn't stay in the state because the bench warrant for my arrest was probably still in place. A lousy, stinking accident; and everybody knew it. A stupid argument over some drunk Joe accusing me of looking at his woman too long. He swings at me. I hit him once. His head hits the edge of the bar. The state nails me for involuntary manslaughter. Some high-priced lawyer my mother hired said, Don't worry, a clean record, no prior arrests, they'll dismiss the charges. Sure, for white men like him—no charges. But the court already had my butt in jail with bail set at an outrageous five hundred thousand. Ten percent down, said the bail bondsman. The only thing she had was her home—free and clear—after thirty years. So her hundred percent went into their ten percent. And if I could have believed in the system the way she did, I wouldn't have run. But I hung out in the streets enough to convince myself they were gonna give me time. How much time, I don't know. Not as much as they would if the dead man was white—but some time. And I felt that any time locked up like an animal would've killed me. My mother knew that, so she put up her house. I knew it, too, and so I ran.

I left Pine Acres Cemetery with another promise to myself. I can't undo the past, but I would find some woman, somewhere, and make her life happy. I would be the father I never had; I would act like the man I'd finally grown up to be. First, I wanted to meet my own father. An only child, like me, whenever Mama talked about her home in Tennessee, it was always a story about her father and mother; about the two nosy spinsters who lived up the hill who always spied on her; but never about *my* father. "Your father wasn't the marrying type," she said, "and so I never bothered to tell him about you." And that was it. It's how she answered every question I had about him. And if I pressed, she'd get angry: "Ain't I been taking good care of you? If you gotta worry, worry about what you got, not about what could never be." But this time that wasn't enough.

Rock Vale is such a small place there are no passenger trains to serve it. I took the long bus ride that ended at a ramshackle depot with a Coke machine, yellowing schedules tacked to the wall, and no full-time clerks. If the station's closed when you're ready to come back, pick up your return ticket from the hardware store, the bus driver said. No pictures. No letters. How was I ever going to find this man? But I did have his name: Butch Fuller. So if he hadn't moved or he wasn't dead, the post office needed to be the first place for me to start.

"For a minute when I looked up, I thought you was Butch," the postal clerk said. "You're sure his spitting image."

The road to my father's house was long, dusty, and hot. Dried weeds and wilting wildflowers flanked each side. Sweat glued my short-sleeved shirt to my back. One of my best shirts. And my polished loafers were covered with grit. The man sat in a cane-backed chair on the porch of a small bungalow. The house looked about two months away from needing a fresh coat of paint; and what passed for a front lawn was a tangle of weeds and sweet grass. I stood at the front gate and looked up into a mirror that changed my image into that of a man thirty years my senior: the same tall thin frame; the same cinnamon-colored skin. Butch Fuller got up from the chair and came to the edge of his porch.

"It's been a long walk," he said. "Would you like a cool drink?"

"I'd appreciate it."

I never left the gate as he went inside to return with a pitcher of lemonade; sweat beading on the glass looking so inviting my throat ached.

"Boy, have enough sense to come on up out of the sun. Since black means poor in these parts, you don't need to get any poorer."

"That sounds like an old joke," I said.

"A very old joke. I told it that one day when I was walking to the cane fields with your mama. How is Mattie?"

"She's dead."

And right then and there, for some ungodly reason, I began to cry. He did me the great favor of ignoring my tears as he poured me a tall glass of his lemonade.

"From the time I was eighteen," he said, "the doctors told me I couldn't have no children. Something about my sperm count. But I knew you had to be mine because I was your mama's first man."

"Maybe you weren't her last," I said, needing to hurt him in some way.

"Last until you were born."

And probably the last after, I thought. I couldn't remember my mother going out more than two times with any man. She made me her life.

"I went to see Mattie after I heard she was pregnant. I was so glad about you proving the doctors wrong that I was foolish enough to start thinking I could ask her to marry me. But her old man wouldn't let me see her. And later he even lied about where she had gone. Your grandfather was a hard, hard man. But I guess he did her—and me—a favor. We was no more meant to be together than a rooster and a goldfish."

"And all these years, you never wondered about me?" I asked.

"I wondered."

"We coulda been starving . . ."

"You coulda been, but you weren't."

"How in the hell would you know?"

"If you came here thinking I was gonna help you with your pain, you're wrong, so stop it. I'm sorry Mattie's passed away but I got no regrets about how I treated her. Then again, maybe you do."

"So I'm your only son?"

"My only child."

"You never married?"

"I ain't the marrying type."

And it went on like that for a good hour, me asking questions and him answering them, but never volunteering any more information about himself. I don't know what I was really trying to find out. What did I want to leave with? Maybe, that way deep down, in spite of the years, he had loved me.

"You take what life gives you," Butch Fuller said, as I got up to go. "It gave me a son I was never to know; and it gave you a father who . . ."

"Who in this whole hour," I exploded, "never *once* asked me my name. My mother was right, it was better to think of you dead."

"I ain't needed to ask your name, Basil. I've been turning it over in my mind since the day you was born. Have a safe trip, Son."

He gave me directions for getting to the house where my mother grew up. The place was a total mess and it looked like a dozen children—different shades of brown—lived there. They were playing in the dirt front yard; climbing up the pillars of the leaning porch. And I saw a few standing behind the broken screen door of the house; all of them barefoot and one of them a toddler wearing only a dirty diaper. "Mama, Mama," they called, "there's a man at the gate."

She came out, and I knew instantly that she was alone. One baby holding onto the frayed hem of her housedress and another balanced on her hip. This is what happens without a man in the house, I thought. I made my excuses and left quickly.

And I swore, once again, that I would not be that kind of man. I was going to be there for my children, that is, if I could have any. What Butch Fuller had talked about gave me concern. Sometimes the condition of low sperm counts can be passed on. And after a battery of tests, the doctors confirmed that was exactly the case. Fathering children would be almost impossible for me. My birth was more than a miracle. On the spiritual side, then, I was here on earth for a reason. And I decided that reason was to be a solid family man. Women, for whatever reason, always considered me handsome. And I never had a problem finding new girl-friends; but this time I was looking for a wife. I began thinking about the women in my past; why we'd broken up. And nine times out of ten, it was because they asked for a com-mitment—or had that look in their eyes that they soon would—and I took off.

And this is where I'll never understand women in a hun-dred million years. I began asking out a few who worked with me at the umbrella factory. I'd take them to nice restau-rants or a show at the Gazebo Theater, and to save time I'd tell them on the first date—or no later than the second—that I was looking for a commitment. I wanted a family and if I couldn't have my own kids, I'd adopt. You might have thought I'd just told them I was the Boston Strangler. I was lying, they all swore, this was just some new line to get them to bed. Had I talked about sex? No. Had I even talked about the bedroom in my new apartment? No. So what in the hell was wrong with them?

I learned quickly that women thought something was very wrong with a man who talked about wanting a commitment before *they* brought up the subject. And even if they did bring it up, for you to agree too quickly made you a loser. A lot of games were out there; you'd go dizzy trying to figure it out. Sure, maybe women had a lot of bad experiences with men to make them that cautious. But I saw that black men weren't the only reason for the mess black women were in. Women yell about finding a man to settle down with; but when one comes along they put him through a lot of crap before they believe. I thought about what advice my mother might give me if she were still alive. "Hang in there, Son. There's light at the end of the tunnel." And what I found at the end of the tunnel was Helen.

She was the boss's secretary. And at first I figured she was out of my league. My mother had sent me to good schools; but I dropped out of college after one semester and here she was working on her master's degree. She wasn't what you'd call a pretty woman but I found her attractive enough: nut-brown skin, short natural hair, and a really nice body—small at the waist and full in the hips— just the way I liked it.

The best thing about her was that she had a good sense of humor. She sounded like a crystal bell when she laughed. And I used my reputation as a charmer to keep her laughing. Sure, we both knew that after only three months of seeing each other it was too early to talk about a true commitment;

but at least the idea of it didn't frighten her away as it had some of the others.

When she began to inch me into her private life, I knew we'd gotten over the first hurdle successfully. We double-dated with Helen's best friend and her husband. She told me later that her girlfriend liked me, and I thought, hallelujah, that's the second hurdle. Never underestimate the power of those girlfriends. They can help to tear you down or build you up with just two phone calls. And finally we had dinner with her parents, both of them dentists. It never made me very popular at school, Helen said, and there were the bells again as she laughed. After she took me to dinner with her parents, I knew it was time to tell her the full story about my past. And I decided to do it that Sunday after we went to church—yes, she even had me going to church—but that was the Sunday that my life turned around and spun in a different direction.

It was Palm Sunday and Sinai Baptist was packed. A Reverend Moreland Woods was the preacher and with his reputation of putting on a good show, the building meant to hold five hundred had twice as many for that morning service. And it was a good service, full of the fire that Woods was noted for. Two pews ahead of us, off to the left, was a young girl with two little boys. I guessed their ages correctly: four and six; and I knew their names because every time one would fidget, the young girl would yank an arm and talk so loudly it could be heard back in our pew. Stop it, Jason. Stop it, Eddie. And they weren't doing anything but being little boys. Helen noticed it as well as I did and just shook her head.

"Do you know that girl?" I asked.

"Unfortunately, I do. It's my cousin, Keisha, and she's bad news. I hate the way she treats her kids."

"Her kids? She looks young enough to be their sister."

"Like I told you, bad news. I'll fill you in later."

At the end of the service when Keisha turned around, she noticed Helen and yanked the two boys from the pew and came toward us. A mellow yellow as we used to say in the streets. Her hair was cornrowed with extensions that fanned her shoulders. Her dress was too short and her perfume was loud. She looked sixteen but later it turned out she was barely twenty. And with her children actually being four and six years old, it meant that she'd started at fourteen. She fought the crowd to catch up with us at the door.

"Hey, Cuz."

Helen was barely civil and trying to get us away as quickly as possible.

"And who's this?" Keisha asked. "He's kinda cute, where'd you find him?"

Helen was inching us away, mumbling something about work. Then little Eddie looked up at me with large brown eyes that could break your heart and asked, "Are you my daddy?"

"No, it ain't your daddy." Keisha hit him so hard I winced. The boy started crying, she tried to shut him up as he cried even harder, and the whole thing was turning into a scene.

"When I get you home you're really gonna get it," she said to the boy. "I'm sick of you doing this and embarrassing me."

"Don't blame the child, maybe I look like his father."

"He don't know his damn father. His father is a . . ."

"That's the way you talk," Helen jumped in, "coming straight out of church?"

"Helen, just get off my back. We're out of here." As she tried to drag the children away, I stopped her and knelt down so I could look them in the eyes.

"Hi, my name is Basil. And if I were your daddy, what kinda stuff would you like me to do?"

They looked up at their mother, asking her silently if it was okay to answer.

"Go on," Keisha said, "don't you hear the man talking to you?"

"Come on, help me out," I said to the boys. "What kinda things would you like to do?"

"A real daddy would take us to the circus," Jason, the older one, finally answered.

"And what about you, Brown Eyes?" I said to Eddie as I took out my handkerchief and wiped the tears from his face.

"Nuthin'."

"Nothing? You mean a real daddy would do nothing with a great kid like you?"

"I ain't nuthin'."

I wanted to get up and strangle their mother. Put my hands around her throat and just shake her until she got some good sense in her head.

"Excuse me, mister," their mother said, "but we gotta go now."

"It's a good thing, your taking them to church," I said.

"If I didn't my mama would kill me. And who's gonna baby-sit when I need to go out?"

I looked at Helen and she was really teed off. She wanted to get out of there. But something about that kid's brown eyes and the way he hung his head fixed me to the spot.

"Helen," I said, "would you mind if we took the boys to the circus?"

"Today?"

"No, not today. The circus is gonna be in town for another two weeks."

"Basil, you know how much I have to do with working and school—I don't know if I could find the time."

"But if *I* could find the time . . ."

"Do what you want."

Keisha was only too happy to think that someone was going to take them off her hands for a day. It was alarming how easily she agreed. She and Helen weren't that close, what if I were a pervert she'd just handed her kids off to?

I took the boys to the circus the following Saturday. Circuses are really for the children in us all. The raw smell of excitement and the crush of the crowds is an adventure in itself. And then for the boys to see the acrobats, spinning and cycling and swinging fifty feet in the air . . . I would've given anything if life was going to allow them to keep the look on their faces that day: the wonder and the magic of watching the impossible done again and again. Jason drank it all up like a sponge, but little Eddie needed convincing that the tigers weren't going to eat him.

"Brown Eyes, don't worry, you're safe. Tigers don't like

sugar and you've already had two cones of cotton candy, caramel popcorn, and a double ice cream cone. That tiger's gonna take a good long look at you and say, 'No way.'"

"Jason ain't had as much ice cream as me, so the tiger might eat him up. But I guess that's okay."

I took two very happy and very tired little boys back to their mother's that evening. They were loaded down with the junk they sell at those events, which seems so magical at the moment: plastic flashlights for spinning in the dark, clown masks, and for little Eddie a stuffed toy tiger. And he kept that toy tiger until the very end.

The next week I took them to a baseball game and the week after that to the indoor rodeo that was coming through town, because Jason said he wanted to be a horse when he grew up. I was hoping that the rodeo would convince him that a horse's life was not that easy.

The more I saw the boys the further apart Helen and I drifted. Each time I asked her to come along and each time she had an excuse. I knew how difficult it was to be keeping a double schedule since I'd done it; but she could have least made it one time with me and the boys. She had gotten it into her head that I was using the children to get to Keisha, which was totally foolish, she was hardly my type. "Why blame the kids for their mother?" I kept asking.

"I see where you're heading, Basil, and there's nothing waiting for you but trouble. Maybe you aren't interested in Keisha but the closer you get to those children, the more difficult it's going to be to leave."

"You know, Helen, we keep talking and talking about the

situation with young black men. They're an endangered species; they're a lost generation; on and on . . . I can't solve the problems of a whole generation; but there are two little kids right here who I can help. So why not? Why couldn't I stay in their lives forever—why couldn't we both?"

"That sounds like a marriage proposal," she said and smiled.

"The closest I'll get to one—yeah."

"The answer is no, Basil."

"Well, thanks for giving it some thought."

"Basil, if I marry you—or any man—I'll want to have my own children. And as far as Keisha's concerned she believes she's dong a great job as a mother. So what if Welfare has become her permanent man? It was like that with her mother and it's going to keep going . . . The way she thinks, there's nothing wrong with it at all."

"Unless someone breaks the cycle for her. And here's a chance. Helen, I believe I can make a difference in the lives of those boys."

"Well, good luck. But to truly make a difference, you're going to have to be there every day. And that means Keisha."

I thought Helen was wrong, and selfish, and a lot of things. And I wasn't sure that I could even give her children. But here were two children ready-made for me. Children who needed a man in their lives. But getting around Keisha was the problem. Sometimes she promises I could take the boys out and when I show up at the apartment, she doesn't let them go. That starts the kids crying; the crying starts her to yelling; and we're all standing there in a mess.

But it was little Eddie who finally solved the problem for me. It was one of our "baby-sitting" days. I would stay in with the boys when Keisha wanted to go out on the weekends, so I came in that evening with a bucket of popcorn and two videos: One was *Bambi*—my choice—and the other was some kind of horror thriller—*Nightmare on Elm Street, Part 52*—their choice.

As usual Keisha was decked out in a dress too tight for her plump body and smelling like a perfume factory. I knew it cost close to a hundred dollars every other month to keep her hair braided so neatly with those extensions, but she was always saying that she never had the money to take the kids anywhere. No kissing them good-bye; no instructions for me as far as putting them to bed on time—just a quick "See ya" and she's out the door. Sometimes to come back that night; most of the times not. And once she left me stuck with them for two days and I had to call into work. I was furious over that because it also meant that the kids had missed a day of school.

But this night I'm nodding off to sleep as the horror film plays. I was trying to hang in there, but how many times can you watch someone chopped by an ax murderer? Little Eddie is curled up, fascinated, on one side of me and Jason is on the other.

"Daddy, Daddy . . ." Jason pulled my ear to wake me up. "We're getting to the good part."

"He's not our daddy," little Eddie said, "he's our best friend."

"No," Jason said, "he's a daddy."

"No, no—" little Eddie was close to tears. "Daddies go away. Daddies go away."

No, I thought, not this time. Not ever again.

It took a little under a month for me to convince Keisha that we should get married. The thing that concerned her was my age. At twenty, like she was, someone close to thirty-five seemed ancient. But once she found out about my bank account, she had no more problems with my age than she did with the fact that a bench warrant was hanging over my head in another state. Most of her men had been in—or were just getting out of—jail. "I'm doing this for my kids," she said. "I know they need a father and I think you'd be a good one." I insisted on new clothes for the boys the day we went down to City Hall. It was very clear to both of us that I wasn't marrying Keisha, I was marrying her boys. And the next time we went to City Hall it was for me to adopt them officially. Jason Michael and Eddie Michael—mine forever.

In six months she had almost run through the forty-seven thousand dollars. Her new Cadillac set me back close to thirty right away. Add to that the credit card bills for the new living-room furniture, hundreds of dollars for clothes and God knows what else because I didn't see where she'd spent it for much else in the house. I guess I should be honest and include the gifts she was giving her men.

It was not a marriage involving love between us; and so I never questioned the nights she spent out. If she respected me enough to lie, I was fine with that. And she did respect and even feared me a little. I stopped her from hitting my boys—

for any reason. You don't always have to discipline a child with your hands. And I stopped her from telling them they were nothing when she was angry with them. It was a home where I was definitely the boss; and as that old blues song goes— paying the cost to be the boss, because I was back to working double shifts at the umbrella factory. I wanted to build a college fund for the boys. Something Keisha just didn't see the need for doing. A high school dropout, her dreams for them ended with them finishing high school and going out on their own. My dreams for them ended on the other side of the universe. They could be *anything* they wanted, I kept telling them. And Daddy's gonna be right there to cheer you on.

"Don't promise them too much," Keisha said. "They'll grow up and be disappointed. I wanted to be a teacher and look at me."

"It's not too late. You can still go back to school."

"No, I stopped dreaming like that long ago. My kids are my life now."

Two years into the marriage—Jason was eight and little Eddie was six—I discovered she was bringing men into our home. "Uncle Penny came to see us again," Eddie said when I got home from work. Penny had been one of her boyfriends before he went to jail for crack possession. And so we had yet another fight—behind a closed bedroom door. Maybe some of this was my fault. Maybe if I'd concentrated on being as good a husband as I did a father, I could have saved the marriage.

"I will kill you," I said softly, "if you bring scum into my home around these boys again."

And there she was, ranting and raving, denying it all. But this time denial wasn't enough. "I'm the one who'll do the killing," she said. "I'm gonna kill Eddie for lying on me."

"You aren't doing anything to him. You'll keep your damn hands off my kids."

"Your kids? They ain't your kids. Since when you man enough to have any kids. You hardly ever touch me. They told me not to marry some old ass like you." And then her eyes narrowed as she went for the jugular. "For all you know, Penny might be their real father. And even if he ain't, he's sure as hell better in bed than you are."

God help me, I hit her. And God help us both, because her eyes told me that's exactly what she wanted. She bounced back up, coming at me swinging with both hands. I warded her off and shoved her on the bed. I held her body down with my own and pinned her arms over her head.

"We've gotta stop this, Keisha, do you hear me? We've gotta stop."

"You piece of shit," she yelled, and kept raging. It was a long stream of curses from her: You mother this—you mother that—. With this type of treatment, she'd finally come alive. It made me sick to my stomach that *this* is what she understood. And I knew the kids must be hearing us—even behind a closed door.

"Keisha, what do you want from me, huh? We can't go on like this."

She was finally calming down. "I want you to get the hell out of my life," she said.

"Okay, I'll take the boys and go."

"Man, are you outta your mind? You ain't taking my kids nowhere."

"Legally they're mine as well as yours."

"We'll see about that. We'll just see."

The next week at quitting time two detectives showed up at my job with a bench warrant for my arrest. I didn't try to lie. I didn't ask them Who? Why? or How? I had just one question: Can I go home and say good-bye to my boys? Maybe one of the cops was a father, or maybe both, but they let me do it. To this day, I don't know if that was the right thing or not. Either way it was going to break my heart. When we got to the apartment, I rang the bell because my hands were shaking too much to use my keys. After several rings, Jason answered the door. He and Eddie were watching television.

"Did you do your homework?" I asked.

"Not yet," they said.

"But Mommy said we could watch TV," Jason added since they knew I never let them until their homework was done.

"Where's your mother now?"

"In the bathroom."

And Keisha would stay locked in that bathroom until I was gone.

"Daddy's got something to tell you," I said. "Cut off the television."

"Who're these men, Daddy?" little Eddie asked. Always the most suspicious of the two boys.

"They're some people that Daddy has to go away with."

"When are you coming back? Tomorrow?"

"No, not tomorrow, but I will be back."

There was a long silence as all of that sank in. And they knew, in the way that children know, that all was not well.

Little Eddie kept staring at the two detectives as Jason asked, "Daddy, is it something we did wrong? I'm sorry about the TV but Mommy said . . ."

"Jason, come here," I said and hugged him so tightly I almost crushed him. "There's nothing that you did wrong. But a long time ago, Daddy made a big mistake and he has to go away now and make it right. But I'll be back.

"Eddie, come here," I said.

"No," he said and kept staring at the detectives.

"Don't you want to give Daddy a kiss good-bye?"

"No," he said. "You're not coming back."

"As God is my judge—I'll be back."

"No," he said. And then he went to get his tiger. We had been calling the toy Tony the Tiger after the cereal commercial. "Take Tony, Daddy—he'll help you beat up these bad men. And then you won't have to go away."

"No, you keep him. To remember me—okay?"

And then what was left of my heart to break— "Daddy, tomorrow is my birthday. I'm gonna be seven."

"I know, Eddie."

"Can't you stay for my birthday and then go away?"

"I wish I could, Eddie." And then I looked at the detectives. "If you let me, I swear to you, I won't run."

They were seasoned cops, those detectives. Tough and

street-smart. But neither of them had dry eyes when they
shook their heads, no.

I left those boys and I did come back after serving six years
for good behavior on a seven-to-fifteen-year count for involuntary manslaughter. Six years of them never getting the
letters or cards I sent. Six years of never being allowed to
visit me. Jason was fifteen years old and Eddie was thirteen
when I finally got out. Keisha was living with Penny, an on-
again-off-again junkie, who'd aged her well past her years.
Jason had already done time himself in juvenile detention
for car theft and aggravated assault. And little Eddie had
built a shell around himself, hard and permanent: He said he
didn't know me. And that he didn't want to.

So I did come back. And am I going to fight for the hearts
of these boys again? I'm going to fight like hell. But the
question that will haunt me for the rest of my life is whether
or not I could have made a difference. Would these things
have happened to them anyway just in the flow of life? But
now I'll never know, will I? I'll never know.

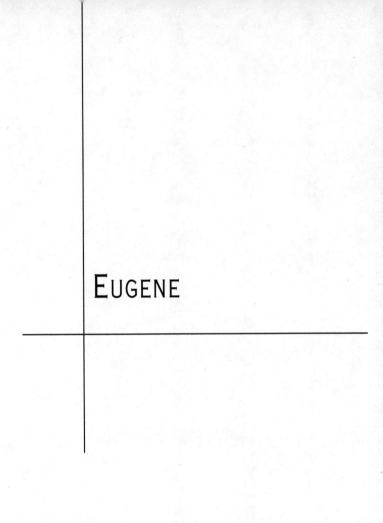

Eugene

Nothing much gets past the super of any building. Like me, he sees 'em come and go. I get up a little past dawn to set out the garbage and sweep any scraps that the wind might have blowed along the street from a few open cans. Preaching over and over to folks that they gotta put the lids down tight don't seem to make a bit of difference; there's always one or two who won't do right for doing wrong. So I'm blamed if there's garbage in the sewers just like I'm accused of harassing them about them closed tops. You can't win for losing most times. But after I've got my garbage set out and the gutters swept, it's time for me to sit on my "throne" and watch the action in the streets. I'm not the type of super that hides from the tenants. Any of them know where they can find me, 'cause they see me right there, sitting on an old garbage can that's pushed up against the wall, taking a sip or two from a small bottle I keep in my back pocket as insurance against the chill in the air most any season.

It's interesting to watch a street unfold as the day dawns. I see the ones coming in from the midnight shifts at hotels, hospitals, the telephone company; and I see the ones leaving to take their places on the morning and afternoon shifts. I know who just got a new job—and who's been fired from one. I know which children are off to school to behave proper and which ones is playing hooky, just waiting for their folks to leave so they can sneak back home. With most of it I just keep counsel with myself and mind my own business. If I notice one child who's skipping school a bit too much, I'll make mention of it to their parents. But I'm not paid to be a cop and stop somebody who is sneaking out and moving because they're

three months back due with the rent; I'm paid to keep these build-
ings from crumbling more than they already are. So it weren't no
secret to me when the Turners were having problems and Eugene
had left Ceil—once again. I figure over the last six years that it's
happened about four or five times. And a nice couple too. It makes
you wonder what it can all be about. Maybe another woman. But
do you keep leaving over and over for the same woman? Maybe it's
a different woman each time; but that don't sit well with me. Eu-
gene ain't a womanizer. One man knows that about another even
if they only speak from time to time like me and Eugene. I guess if
I wanted to take the trouble to listen to Brother Jerome's blues as
Eugene comes and goes, I would get the answer. But that would be
like peeking in through someone's bedroom window. I ain't a
Peeping Tom, I'm a super. And I figure if Eugene wanted me or
anybody else to know his business, he would bring it to us. There's
nothing wrong with his mouth, he can speak for himself.

I've been running around in circles, not knowing
where to begin. There's so much to say to you, Ceil. So
much to explain. But before I begin, you must believe that I
did love you and Serena. I was so proud the day she was
born; it was like a miracle watching you give birth. Can you
remember that about me, with all the other crap that went
on between us, can you at least remember that I was in the
delivery room that day? Yeah, I know, crying and laughing at

the same time. Acting like a stone fool, but proud, sweetheart, so proud of the daughter you gave me. It made me believe that we could really make it together after all.

Ceil, if you were here, instead of totally out of my life, off in San Francisco, I know what you'd be asking. You asked it so many times during our marriage, in one way or another: Why? Why did I keep leaving? We'd get a little bit ahead, a few dollars in the bank, start taking long walks together on the "nice" side of town, daydreaming about moving out of Brewster Place into that red brick house we were going to buy one day: a large yard for Serena; complete with a swing set and sliding board. A large workshop in the basement for me.

"And what do I get that's large?" you'd tease.

"You mean, besides me?"

"You better believe it—besides you."

"How about a large woodshed? I can take you out back for a spanking when you start to acting up."

"In your dreams, buddy. How about a large bathroom. Jacuzzi? Steam room? A tub so deep I could almost drown in it."

"A tub big enough for two? I can buy that."

"Even big enough for three."

"Getting a little kinky there, huh?"

They were wonderful walks, Ceil. And wonderful dreams. All bolstered by the fifteen hundred dollars we'd managed to put away. Hard dollars, saved with your cutting corners on the grocery bill and never buying yourself new clothes. Saved with my working overtime, sometimes double time at the docks. But then I'd take exactly half of whatever we had in the savings; and then I would leave, wouldn't I? And the hardest part about packing my clothes was the sight of those old dresses hanging in the closet. Why did I keep leaving? Baby, that's not the right question. It never was. The question is, Why did I keep coming back?

faggot

And you can believe it or not, but I loved you. I had loved you from the first time I saw you, racing past my aunt's house in Tennessee. Those long, brown legs almost flying over the dirt roads in Coral Rock, hardly stirring up dust. That lean, boyish body built for speed. The only girl allowed to play stickball with us; even having team captains fight over you because you weren't only fast but strong. Putting you out in center field meant that nothing short of a home run got away. I was fourteen. And you were only twelve. A whisper of a girl who could leap and who could run; but I knew I wanted you in my life when the years showed me that you could also dream.

"Can we be pen pals when my vacation is over?" I asked that first summer.

"Sure," you said, "I like to write letters."

And what letters they were: your plans to leave Tennessee one day and go off "to explore the world." Can black girls be airplane pilots? you asked in an early letter. I hope so because then I could just fly around the whole world and see it at one time.

And when it was time for my vacation again, we'd go fishing together or picking dewberries and talk about your plans to be *special*.

"That's all I want, Eugene, not money or stuff like that, I just want to be special."

"You're already special. You can run faster than any boy in town, except, maybe, Bug Eye. You can climb higher. And God knows, you've got a great pitching arm."

"But that only makes me special here; and this is a small place. I'm leaving one day and that's when I want to . . . Well, I don't know exactly what I want, but in a bigger place . . ." And your eyes would get that look that meant I wasn't there and Coral Rock wasn't there—just you and the future.

"Come on," you'd say, snapping out of it, "race you to that cottonwood."

"You're gonna lose this year, Ceil, see how long my legs have gotten."

"So a small bet? I win, you buy the RCs. You win, you buy the RCs to celebrate your victory."

"Gal, do I look that stupid to you?"

"Uh-huh."

Before I could blink an eye you were off and running. And so each summer's end when I had to return to Pittsburgh, I was haunted with the memory of a tall, brown-skinned girl whose breath smelled of lemon candy and whose skin was polished by the touch of the wind. I finally married you at eighteen; took you away from Coral Rock; and proceeded slowly, very slowly, to ruin your life.

faggot

I met Bruce on my first job at the docks. He was head fore-man for the company and everything I believed a black man should be: big, dark, and mean. When he said, do something, everyone hopped to do it, even the white boys who liked sit-ting around and telling darky jokes on their lunch hour. Bruce was from the old school; he didn't take much to "good man-agement skills." The way he saw it was: I'm the boss here and the only skill you need is to move your ass when I tell you to—and move it good and quick. He measured how effective he was by how much he was feared, so he rated himself damn good at his job. The company must have felt the same way too because whenever he asked for a raise, he got one. And if any-one mumbled "union," and believe me, it was just a mumble, he called for a speedup. "You see," he told us, "when the union rep gets here, I want him to see how men work; and maybe that'll help me figure out what losers been running be-hind my back and crying for their mama's titty."

Don't mess with Bruce. That was the word on the docks. And don't think you could pull that "brother man" shit on him, the other black longshoremen warned me. If anything, he's harder on our asses than the others. With all this, there was still a waiting list, half a yard long, to work for our com-pany. Because while he had a reputation for being fierce, he was also fair. And the docks were no place for a man who wanted an easy time. It was heavy, sometimes dirty, work. And if anybody didn't do their job, it was also dangerous. Hauling six, seven tons of cargo from the hold of a ship took teamwork. You worked knowing that a winch could snap, a crate could start swinging wild and cost some man his life. Hard work. And one way or another, you were going to sweat. I didn't complain because I was glad for the work. The docks paid twice as much as any other job I was qualified to do with only a high school education; and I was glad for the money with a new wife and a baby on the way. So when the foreman said, Jump to it, Turner, you better believe I jumped.

But there was always hot coffee and fresh doughnuts for break time; and when we broke at noon, we got our full hour in a lunchroom that he'd wrangled out of the company. Nothing much: a few Formica tables with a used refrigerator and a microwave sectioned off in the rear of an old supply shed. But it made a big difference from other jobs where you sat out in the open on freight crates with the smell of leaking oil and dead fish coming on the breeze from the river. A Lakers' fan, he never said a word about a rusted hoop someone nailed on the rear of the toolshed for the guys who wanted a little one-on-one before it was time to get back to work. He'd even play a quick game himself; although not many wanted to take him on. From the looks of him, you'd never guess that the man was that good at hoops. He was built more like a football player with those huge shoulders and legs like tree trunks. And he played the game like it was football; once he was on defense, he didn't guard—he charged. It took a lot of heart to keep the ball with all two hundred and fifty pounds of solid muscle bearing down on you, grinning wide, talking trash—anything short of attacking your mother—to get your mind off your shot. We played rough and there was no such thing as a foul. Well, maybe if you picked up a lead pipe and hit the point guard upside the head, it might—and I said, might—get him a free throw.

On a scale of one to ten, I was probably a six as a player. I enjoyed watching the other guys as much—if not more—as I did playing. If there was a bet floating and Big Bruce wasn't part of the game, I usually threw my money behind Italian Freddy. When Bruce was part of the game, all bets were off, because it was pretty much a sure thing.

faggot

Practically everyone can look back and remember a day that was to change their life. And that day rarely starts out as anything special. You get up, get dressed, and get hustling to make sure you're not late for work, or school, or whatever. And then out of the clear—it happens: you decide to stop at the newsstand for a pack of gum and end up buying that winning lottery ticket; you're racing across the street to beat a red light and get hit by a taxi making an illegal left turn; or maybe, you're simply chilling out at home when the phone rings . . . and rings . . . and rings . . . But it wasn't a telephone that brought me face-to-face with my fate.

"Hey, Turner, wanna little one-on-one?"

Funny, how I've blocked the exact day but the month looms large in my mind: August. It was what the crew called an easy August. The temperature never reached above eighty and the humidity was low. So you could work without breathing through your mouth to lessen the stench that hung like a cloud over that greasy water. I remember it also being a light workday with only two ships coming in. The men were in a good mood so there had been plenty of takers for a quick lunchtime game around the hoop. Yes, I remember it was August and I remember it was evening.

The wharf lights were just coming on, casting large shadows from the ship docked at our pier and from other piers along the water. And maybe it was payday because a few stragglers were still hanging around, talking about going out for a few drinks. But it was August. And the only weird thing about that day was that twice I caught Bruce staring at me and I remember my heart pounding: Work had been slow all month, was he going to lay me off? Last in; first out.

I heard the basketball hitting the backboard before he stepped out of the shadows, moving closer and closer to the lighted hoop as he sank them—never missing—like a machine—one after the other.

"That is you—isn't it, Turner?"

"How'd you know I was standing here?"

"Eyes in the back of my head, boy, ain't you figured that out yet?" Tah-dump. Tah-dump. The ball hitting the ground in a slow dribble. He pauses, shoots—and makes it. And watching the ball make that perfect arch from his hands to the hoop, it came to me: He knows.

"So whadya say? A little one-on-one?" he asked again.

"Twenty-one wins?"

"Naw, tonight, let's just say the sky's the limit."

"You're gonna crucify me, Bruce."

"Big time."

I wished I had a way to wipe that cocky grin off his face. I pulled off my T-shirt and tied it around my waist.

"Then, again, maybe you won't," I said. "You so big and ugly, that ball's already crying out for a new papa."

"I invented signifying, Turner, so don't start up with me."

"That right? You invented signifying?"

"Damn straight. Your monkey ass was still in diapers when I started playing ball."

We each took a turn at sinking the ball. First man to miss lost control of the ball. Bruce shot again and made it. I shot and made it.

"Know what I can't figure out about you, Turner?"

"I'm all ears."

"Why don't you just pay the bail so your mama can get out of prison?"

"You that scared, Bruce? Dragging my mama into this already—yeah, you must be real scared."

"I ain't scared. Just wondering why you such a cheap-ass bastard?"

"Well, before my mama went to prison, know what she told me?"

"I'm all ears . . ."

"She said, 'Son, never get mad—just get yourself a loaded forty-five.'" I shot again and made it. He shot and missed.

"My ball."

"You ain't keeping it, Turner."

"Watch."

All those afternoons looking on from the sideline gave me a chance to study how each man played. Bruce's weakness was that he couldn't jump. With those huge long arms waving in your face or jabbing you in the side, it was easy to forget that he always dribbled toward the back court to turn and make his shots. The trick was to keep him close to the basket when he was shooting; and to stay between him and the basket when it was time for you to shoot. Just brace yourself for a hard body slam and keep your eyes on the hoop.

Fifteen baskets to twelve—his favor. And we were both sweating like mules. His sweat had a deep musk smell to it that reminded me of lying on my back in the summertime woods of Coral Rock. A bed of dried oak leaves and broken juniper branches—of matted sweet grass and fresh soil. My body ached from being slammed again and again; but it was eighteen to eighteen and his ball. I was hell-bent on keeping him from backing up and positioning to shoot.

Tah-dump. Tah-dump. Tah-dump. He was dribbling fast and low; and I was right there with him.

"Know what I'm gonna do for you, Turner? I'm gonna let you get this point."

"Do me no favors."

"It ain't a favor. Just call it a donation to the handicapped."

Tah-dump. Tah-dump. Tah-dump. His dribble was so fast and perfect, it seemed like the ball was attached to his hand with a rubber band.

"Man, you the one who's handicapped. You can't jump."

"I look white to you?"

"Black as the ace of spades—and you still can't jump."

"Turner, brace yourself for the experience of a lifetime."

And when he left the ground, I went with him. Both of us

floating up past the old rusted hoop. Up toward the rising stars over that greasy muddy river. And when we landed, it was on two corner stools near the window at the Bull & Roses in the financial district.

"My favorite stool," Bruce said. "Sometimes I watch the crowd. Sometimes I check out the street. And that's how I knew. You almost came through the door last week. But the weeks before that, you'd walk past, turn around and come back; walk past, turn around and come back. It ain't took no genius to figure it out."

The bar was smoky and so dense with bodies it took a while to realize that it was filled with nothing but men except for two women at a table near the back. Definitely an upscale place with its mahogany panels, hanging ferns, and the walls covered with huge colored photographs or oil paintings of Spanish matadors fighting bulls or doing victory strolls as they were showered with flowers from screaming fans in the arenas. The patrons, three deep at the bar, can only be described as Wall Street meets the Teamsters with everything that fell in between. The leather trade rubbed shoulders with Brooks Brothers and no one seemed to resent the others' presence. Mostly white but with enough Blacks and Latinos thrown in so that Bruce and I hardly stood out.

"Welcome to the sisterhood," he said and took another swig of his beer.

One of the women at the far table, wearing a low-cut, skintight bodysuit of silver lamé, got up to come toward us. The silvery cloth caught the little bit of light to be found in the room. As she came closer, I made my second mistake by thinking it was a man. I would later understand that Chino was an island unto himself; his own country; his own god. He spent every waking moment thinking of ways to cram his uniqueness down someone's throat. And that night it was going to be me. It was amazing that when he drifted through the crowd it parted for him as if he were the Latino queen he tried so hard to be. He glided up beside Bruce and greeted him, kissing the air on each side of his cheeks.

"Bruce, love. It's been so long."

His reddish curly hair was pinned back with diamond rhinestones. Electric-blue eye shadow. Cinnamon blush. And red pouting lips that whispered so softly you wondered how his words could cut so badly.

"And she sees that you've brought us another virgin. Green meat always fascinates me. Does he have a name?"

"I'm not deaf," I said. "I can speak for myself."

"Ah, touchy, touchy . . . She didn't mean to offend. Her name is Chino—what's yours?"

He stood there in that silver bodysuit, having walked out of my worst nightmares. *This* is what you would think of me. *This* is what I might become. Later, so much later, I would learn that Chino's perfume and paint were nothing but a hiding place to anchor himself somewhere after having managed to put himself nowhere by running away from his true self under a surgeon's scalpel. He grew up believing that he loved men because he was meant to be a woman. It's a long process to change your sex—the battery of psychological tests, the hormone injections, and then finally a series of op-

erations. Coming down to the finish line, he faced the truth
that he didn't really want to be a woman. It was just easier to
handle the world's contempt—as well as his own—to think of
himself as a woman loving men than as a man loving men.
But they had already castrated him when he stopped the op-
erations. And there was no going back. So he moved forward,
caught in limbo, and left to define himself. He took his mu-
tilated, caramel-colored body and dressed it in metallic
bodysuits. He let his hair grow long since it gave him more
options to dress it in rhinestones, feathers, or getting it dyed
to a flaming red or even blond. Perfect nails. Perfect makeup.
He finally decided that since he could be anything—anything at all—he would use each waking breath finding a way
to be seen as more than beautiful—*divine.*

"What if I told you my name was Pete?" I asked.

"You'd be telling a lie. But then again . . ." He drummed his
red painted nails on the bar top. "You do smell . . . married."

"My name is Eugene."

"It's precious. She loves it. Her first Eugene."

"Why do you keep talking about yourself like that?" I asked.

"Like what?" he whispered.

"Like you're somebody else. Like you're not standing
here."

"It's called the third person. I speak of myself in the third
person. Isn't it obvious that there's just too much beauty
here for one person?"

I looked to Bruce for help, but he'd suddenly become interested in watching people walk past the window out on the
street.

"I mean," Chino continued, "how can one person—*one person*—be me?"

"You got me," I said, wishing real hard that I'd gone straight home.

"That's okay, Chino forgives you. But next time bring your eyeglasses . . . No, on second thought, bring your sunglasses. Because the next time you see me, I shall *radiate* for you, Eugene. Just you."

Bruce finally came to my rescue. "All right, that's enough for now, Chino."

"Oh, she didn't mean to imply . . . Is he yours, Bruce?"

"He's a guy from work—and that's it. Now go share your glory with someone else at the other end of the bar."

"But, Bruce, it's so much fun with a virgin."

"You've had your fun. Now get lost."

"Cruel, cruel world. When your friends turn against you. But I forgive, Eugene, I am a well of bottomless mercy."

To my relief, Chino finally drifted off. And when he turned around, I could see the tattoo in blazing silver on his bare back: BORN TO PARTY.

"What does he do for a living?" I asked Bruce.

"He's a prostitute. And watch out for him, he's heavy into S and M. His real hangout is the Purple Cock. Rough trade. This little bit of leather you see in here with these white boys is just playing dress-up in daddy's clothes compared to what Chino's real crowd is about."

"Aren't you worried about AIDS?" I asked.

"Every day."

"And what if you're seen by one of the guys from work?"

"If I'm seen by one of the guys, that means they're in here too, don't it?"

"They could say they were just doing it for laughs."

"I can do the same thing. But why? See, that's the difference between me and you, Turner. I don't give a flying fuck what anybody thinks. It's my time. My money. And my beer."

"Around the docks you never said that you were . . ."

"'Cause nobody's ever asked me."

faggot

He was right. No one ever asked; or even talked about him except to say—very quiet—that he was a mean son of a bitch. But I wasn't like Bruce, I *was* afraid of what you would think of me if I walked into our apartment that very night to tell where I'd been and—more important—to tell you why. I decided, right there, for both of us, that you would hate me. I couldn't bear to think of the contempt that would be in your eyes. I was a man; and you would no longer see me as a man—your man—but as some sort of freak. Yes, Ceil, I decided right then and there that you would hate me as much as I hated myself. And so the lies began . . .

Small lies, like the one I told that night: Just out with the guys for a coupla beers. On to the big lies: We were going to buy a house large enough for our grandchildren to move in, while I no longer imagined having children with you, no less grandchildren. After that first night at the Bull & Roses, when I opened up that part of myself I'd been running from most of my life, I saw our marriage as a trap. You and I both caught in the web of my denial; caught in a two-year-old marriage with no easy out. Somebody was going to bleed from this. And at first, it was only me.

The Bull & Roses wasn't really a cruising bar, more like a neighborhood hangout, but things did happen. For the longest time I never picked up a man there or allowed myself to be picked up. I went there more to relish the possibilities; to convince myself that the guy in the vest and gray suit was normal. The guy in the plaid shirt and jeans was normal. So I, with my sweaty hands wrapped tightly around a bottle of Coors, was just as normal. You're looking at men, Eugene, I kept telling myself, nothing but men. They're aren't freaks. So why did I feel so freaky inside? I would go home, kiss you hello, and then go into the bathroom to put my head down and cry. I turned the water on full force in the sink to cover the sound of my crying. Proof again that there was something wrong with me. Sitting on the closed lid of the toilet, acting like a goddamned baby. Acting like a goddamned . . .

I always ended up getting into the shower and washing myself, rubbing hard with the cloth from top to bottom; shampooing my hair, even using a pumice stone on my feet. All of it like my thoughts had become dirt on my skin. Dirt I could send down the drain as long as the water was running. By the second month of my doing this you began to complain about the gas bill from my using so much hot water.

"Look, Ceil, I don't ask for much around here. Can't I take a damn shower without you on my back?"

"What's wrong with you? I'm not trying to start a fight. I'm just saying . . . Forget it, Eugene. Do what you want. But if you're serious about us saving money, then you've gotta meet me halfway. I haven't bought any new clothes in almost a year and I do my own hair; so the least you could do is . . ."

To avoid any more arguments, I stopped going into the bathroom and running the hot water. The next month you were happy about the reduced gas bill. And the month after that, I was gone.

"What did I do?" you kept saying to me when I called to see how you were. "What did I do?"

"You didn't do anything, Ceil, I just need some space."

"You don't love me anymore?"

Woman, I loved you so much, it hurt. But there was no way to tell you about myself. Do you understand? There was no way. And since I wasn't with you any longer, I could go to the Bull & Roses and ask myself, "How does all of this feel now that I'm a single man?" I didn't make the excuse, like many married men, that it wasn't really cheating as long as it's not another woman. It was cheating; the same secrecy, the same lies. But it felt so right, Ceil. The first time I went home with another man from that bar, it felt so complete. At least, for a short while until the guilt of what I was doing to you came back to wrap itself around my chest and tighten into an iron knot.

I came back the first time when you told me you were pregnant. And I stayed until the baby was born. I named her Serena because I was begging God for peace. But why did I come back the second time? The third time? For the same reason that you never changed the lock on the door: We were meant for each other. So God help us both. And we come to the last time, don't we Ceil? Everything has a last time; and the last time I left was to change both of our lives.

After the fourth time I came back, we had given up the dream that we'd have our own house; be able to leave Brewster Place one day. With my coming and going so much, we were lucky to be able just to hold our own. When I think of all the other things I hated myself for, killing that one dream of yours came very close to the top. But a man gets tired of hating himself, Ceil, and I began to accept there was no way out. And oddly enough, it was Chino, of all people, who helped me to see that a clean break, in the end, would be the kindest thing to do.

Bruce had become a sort of godfather for me as I entered "the life." He said that he didn't want me making the same mistakes he did. There're men out here who will hang you and strip you alive. And that type always smells out someone like you: young, new, and still searching. But if you stay around and stop beating yourself up, you're bound to meet somebody special. I didn't bother to explain to him that I'd already met someone special. I had met you.

If I could consider Bruce a godfather, Chino had become, in his own words, my fairy godmother. Make a wish, Sweet Water, and she will fulfill it. I hated him calling me Sweet Water, and all the more reason why he kept doing it. Chino was determined to get your attention, one way or the other. And if you got him near to closing time at the Bull & Roses, when he was tired of dancing and vamping through the room, you got a conversation that was as close to sensible as he was ever going to come.

"You think I'm a freak, don't you?"

"Chino, I think less about you than any other man in here."

"Red alert. Red alert. She's trying to be serious."

"Okay, when I first met you, I did think that."

"And now?"

"I still think that."

"She walked right into that one, didn't she?"

"With both eyes open."

When you could look beyond the makeup, sequins, and feathers, he had a wonderful laugh. Full and deep—and this time, real.

"You know," I said, "you should think about stopping all that stuff—talking about yourself in the third person. It's cute now, but one day you're gonna get old. And you don't wanna be an old queen with a French poodle who walks around talking to himself."

"Never. And she hates poodles—prissy ass little dogs. If anything it would be a rottweiler."

"An aging queen with a rottweiler? That's sure different."

"Amen. It's supposed to be, Sweet Water. She's going out the same way she came in—flaming. But it's late and she's tired, so let's get serious."

"I'm ready if you are."

"Divorce her, Eugene."

"Who?"

"Your wife. If you love her and the kid, divorce her."

"Who in the hell are you to tell me . . ."

"If you don't make a clean break, you're going to start hating her one day."

"Get the hell away from this table."

Chino got up, looking tired and much older than his

thirty-something years. He threw the feather boa around his neck, and left me the money for his half of the tab.

"And I won't even tell you later that *I* told you so," he said. "And that's right, Sweet Water, in honor of the importance of this moment, I did say *I*."

His advice turned out to be true sooner than I realized. I thought it was only being laid off at the docks that had me so upset about your second pregnancy. Union rules: last hired, first fired—friends with Bruce or not. But it wasn't about being laid off; it was seeing a lifetime of coming and going with the burden of one more child to love. And for some stupid reason, I blamed you for this next baby. You did it to trap me. I tossed and turned in bed for a good many nights. Since I didn't have the guts to tell you, what could I do—what could I possibly do to make you finally change the locks on the door?

I came in the evening that I'd been laid off, slammed the front door, threw my keys on the table, and turned up the stereo loud.

"Eugene, you're home early, huh?"

"You see anybody else sitting here?"

No matter what, I was going to pick a fight. I knew Serena was asleep. If she wasn't, she always toddled toward me each evening I came through the door, holding up her teddy bear—"Hug bear"—and then after I'd hugged the bear—"Hug Serena"—arms reaching out for Daddy; and Daddy reaching out for her; salvation in her soft flesh, her innocence. But that night you refused to say anything about the loud music, you just closed the baby's door. You went into the kitchen and began to prepare dinner. You started the water in the kitchen sink, letting it run and run as you cleaned the rice. Somehow, the sound of the running water made me furious. More furious than the slump in your shoulders as you resigned yourself to take whatever punishment that I would deliver.

"I lost my job today," I shot at you as if you'd been the reason. "So now, how in the hell I'm gonna make it with no money, huh? And another brat coming here, huh?"

The water kept running and running. And I kept going. "I'm fucking sick of never getting ahead. Babies and bills, that's all you good for."

You placed the wet pot of rice on the burner and turned to me defeated.

"All right, Eugene, what do you want me to do?"

We both knew what I wanted you to do, but neither of us had the courage to spell it out. But I was praying for you to find enough courage, Ceil, to throw my ass out the door—a door with new locks.

"Well, look," you continued, "after the baby comes, they can tie my tubes—I don't care."

I saw how hard it was for you to swallow that lie.

"And what the hell we're gonna feed it when it gets here— air? With you and two kids on my back, I ain't never gonna have nothing." I grabbed you by the shoulders, shouting into your face. "Nothing, do you hear me, nothing!"

Did I know you were going to get an abortion? You never mentioned it. And I didn't ask. Instead I promised myself, once again, to be the man you needed me to be.

This time I lasted six months. "If you love her and the kid, divorce her." Good advice from Chino that I didn't listen to. And if I had, I wouldn't be a murderer and our daughter would still be alive. And now to get on with it, right, Ceil? To get on to the last time we saw each other. The last fight.

Everything I've said so far has been leading up to this. One day of talking? A thousand days of talking? I don't know how long I've been going on, but there I was packing my bags and lying again; lying as fast as I could stuff T-shirts and jeans into my suitcase.

"You know, baby, this is really a good break after me being out of work for so long. And hell, Maine ain't far. Once I get settled on the docks up there, I'll be able to come home all the time."

"Why can't you take us with you?"

"'Cause I gotta check out what's happening before I drag you and the kid up there."

"I don't mind. We'll make do. I've learned to live on very little."

"No, it just won't work right now. I gotta see my way clear first."

"Eugene, please."

I cringed listening to you begging me; I wasn't good enough for you to wipe your shoes on. And I saw my prayers answered when I looked into your eyes and saw all my lies; all my leavings; and the baby you gave up. She'll hate me soon, I thought with my heart breaking, She'll hate me very soon and finally change the damn locks on the door.

"No, and that's it," I yelled, flinging my shoes in the suitcase.

"Well, how far is it? Where did you say you were going?"

"I told ya—the docks in Newport."

"That's not in Maine. You said you were going to Maine."

"Well, I made a mistake."

"How could you know about a place so far up? Who got you the job?"

"A friend."

"Who?"

"None of your damned business!"

This lie became all my lies. And I was drowning in them. I had to get away quick, I couldn't bear much more. And in all this time, we never thought about Serena. Why didn't we wonder about the baby? Because she was safe in the living room, playing with her plastic blocks. She wasn't crawling under the kitchen table, banging on the chrome legs with a block until she found a fork under there, dropped and forgotten. She wasn't trying to poke her fingers into the slits of the electric socket—she was playing in the living room, safe. She wasn't banging against the electric socket with that fork. No, we never thought about the baby—until she finally managed to edge the thin prongs of the fork toward the electric socket.

I was rushing around the bedroom, trying to cram as much as I could into my suitcase. I slammed down the top and yanked it off the bed, surely looking like the trapped animal I felt myself to be.

"You're lying, aren't you? You don't have a job, do you? Do you?"

"Look, Ceil, believe whatever the fuck you want to. I gotta go."

You grabbed the handle of my case. "No, you can't go."

"Why?"

There was a long, long silence and then finally: "Because I love you."

"Well, that ain't good enough."

You let the suitcase go before I jerked it away and stood there, looking at me. And I saw in your eyes, finally, the beginning of the end. Then we heard the scream from the kitchen.

What did I feel after I murdered Serena? You must understand that I did not dare to feel anything at all. Anything. I hid behind two masks to get through the next few days with neighbors and your friends. If they tried to console me, it was the strong-black-man mask. And if they came too late to blame me for what I'd already blamed myself for, it was the fuck-you-all-who-gives-a-shit mask. But inside I was feeling nothing; and I mean that, Ceil—nothing at all. Do you know how much work that took? After they came to take the baby to the morgue and you to the hospital for sedation, since my bags were already packed, I checked into a cheap hotel. And waited. And waited. And waited. Surely, if there were a God, He would answer my one prayer: Take the rest of my life in exchange for only the last forty-eight hours. Don't let them bury my baby yet—just give me back the last forty-eight hours.

I lie there on that lumpy mattress—no booze, no drugs— bargaining with God: I didn't even need the whole forty-eight hours. Just forty-one hours and thirty minutes. Surely He could find some use for all those years I was willing to give Him in exchange for a lousy, stinking, goddamned forty-one hours and thirty minutes. All right, forty hours and ten minutes. Okay, I'll even shave it back to thirty-nine hours and fifty minutes. Don't bury my baby yet. Just thirty-nine hours and fifty minutes and I could still make it home.

By the morning of the funeral I was down to thirty-eight hours and fifteen minutes. I missed the services because I was still thinking of a way to redo it all. Somehow make it right. And only I would have to make it right. There was no God worth shit who couldn't give me thirty-eight hours and ten minutes. The whole damn universe to rule—and all I wanted was a little more than thirty-eight hours. But nobody worked with me—God, you, the funeral director—nobody. You buried my baby that day. And in order not to kill myself, I had to think of how I was going to make it through the next thirty or forty years not feeling anything—anything at all.

But I knew the pain was circling and moving around me; making the air so thick I moved from place to place in that hotel room as if I were underwater. Everything slowed down: the way I moved my head, shuffled my feet. Letting nothing inside, the pain could only be worn outside. It bent my back; it sagged my shoulders; weighed down my arms and bowed my head. If I wasn't careful, if I let down my guard just a little, it would get inside and force me to kill myself. You don't wait for pain like this to go away; because it only gets worse with time. I had either to ignore it—ignore that overnight my hair was turning gray—or replace it with something else. Could there be a greater pain than this? I didn't know but I was going to try and find out.

The bartender at the Bull & Roses told me that Chino had

just gone home. And since he was a prostitute his address was common knowledge. I wasn't going to him for sex, I was looking as hard as I could for redemption. It seemed I stood for hours in front of his apartment door before trying to knock. I saw my hand ball into a fist; I saw it striking the steel door repeatedly, but moving underwater I barely heard anything.

He opened the door in a long silk kimono that flowed to the ground and opened just to the navel. Its gray color was repeated as a theme throughout the entire apartment. Gray silk brocade on the couch and the easy chairs; light silver draperies that were gathered into sections so that the gauzy material moved gently with each small breeze from the open windows. The raw silk carpet was slick under my shoes and each step I took left a slight indentation that turned each footstep, for just a moment, into a darker shade of grey.

"Chino . . ."

"Yes, pet?" His voice as always a whisper.

He waited patiently for me to continue. Neither of us said another word as I stood in the middle of the living room, I don't know, with some insane hope that he could read my mind and save me from voicing the favor I needed.

"Chino . . ."

He draped himself over the divan, the long sleeves of the gray kimono blending into its cushions.

"Chino, they buried my baby today."

"Beasts."

I sank to my knees in front of the divan, dry sobs vibrating my body, and my head touching the incredible smoothness of his carpet.

"Chino . . ."

"Enough said."

This was a man who was used to satisfying desires. And so he knew I had come for redemption—I had come searching for his type of pain to replace mine. He reached behind the divan and grasped the handle of the leather whip. Nine lashes that ended with metal tips.

"I have them made of silk ribbons," he said. "I have them made of rope. But you didn't come here to play."

He led me into a small room that was tiled from floor to ceiling—all gray tiles.

"It's easier for washing off the blood," he said. "Assume the position." And so I pulled off my shirt and went to my knees. He whipped me until his arms grew tired, specks of my blood covering everything but the tiled ceiling.

"Enough, Sweet Water?"

"No."

"Please . . ."

"No."

So he kept on trying to stomach the work that was replacing my pain. Little by little replacing it.

"Chino . . ."

"Surely, it's enough, Sweet Water."

"No," I said through a throat that was like sandpaper. "I'll tell you when to stop . . . I'll tell you when to stop . . ."

MORELAND T. WOODS

The lid on the garbage can where I usually sit can get awful hot in the summer season, and I'll often trade it for a seat on the top step of 316, the building closest to the wall which gives a little bit of shade. When summer comes to this street, our children bloom like flowers. They crowd the steps and hang off the railings in all colors of shorts and T-shirts plastered on ebony, gold, and nut-brown legs and arms. Brewster Place practically glows with the energy from their yelling and jumping and racing bicycles from one end to the other. Every day some of these little ones will turn on the fire hydrant to give themselves—and any passerby—a real good shower. And there they are, running down the steps in their bathing suits as the swirling water cleans the gutter and gives them a sidewalk beach to play on just a few feet from home. The adults will call from the windows or the stoops to protest lightly but they welcome the cool spray that drifts through the street. It can get awfully hot in a place with no trees and no grass.

There are two things that the folks on this street take dead serious: their children and their religion. 'Cause any hope they have for the future is all wound up in them two things. Most of 'em are Baptists or Methodists with a little Pentecostal sprinkled into the mix. Not so many Catholics though. I guess I saw my last Catholic here when Mrs. Rubini passed away. A nice old Italian lady who hung in here to the end, even when the street had turned mostly black. But much of what I remember my grandfather telling me keeps me a little cautious about what any religion might have to say. But I'm not as bitter as he was; I figure that a little bit of God is within us all, but it shows more on some than others. No, I don't make it much to church but I do enjoy the revival meetings that always take place in the summer. A big blue-and-white tent goes up on a vacant lot about three blocks down and you can practically sit in your apartment and hear a good dose of their singing and clapping. It does something to you inside even though you might think that you'd left God behind or vice versa. Just like Brother Jerome's playing: you might believe that you've managed the pain, that it's over, until his music seeps down deep into that place where it's hiding and stirs it up again.

I can almost clock the time of year that Reverend Woods will show up on this block in his dark blue Cadillac. He makes visits to the members of his congregation just a week or so before the revival meeting sets up its tent. I guess it's to put in a good word for Sinai Baptist and to remind them where their loyalty belongs. Reverend Woods is sure to lose a few members to the revivalists each year no matter what he does. But he's a smart man who knows that you catch a dripping pipe before the whole thing busts. Something about him, though, seems too smart. And I ain't talking about the fancy suits and car. It's like his soul's been greased with Vaseline and nothing much really sticks there, nothing much is real. Is the man making a game of religion? No, I don't think that. But I do think that if your soul's so smooth it can just glide you right on through life, there's no way to understand what the common man is going through. And if you can't understand that, how do you help him to heal the little wounds inside? The little wounds that can grow into big wounds, that can grow so fast they take over a life? I'll bet my bottom dollar that the Reverend Woods ain't never felt a wound like that. And if a preacher can't feel his

own insides, how can he feel yours? Just an observation. I'm not
trying to be no genius or schoolteacher. When the weather turns
this hot, it's enough work just to be yourself.

The Right Reverend Moreland T. Woods had a quar-
rel with God. Big time.

He saw himself as Job: mistreated, misunderstood, put
upon for no good reason. And when that played out he liked
Jeremiah, also misunderstood and sent to a hardheaded people. And there was also Jonah—a prophet harassed and
without honor; or even John the Baptist, alone and crying in
the wilderness. Reverend Woods loved the J's in the Bible;
all of them fitting, he believed, his current situation in life.
Why couldn't the deacons' board just go along with him and
agree to building a larger church? Sinai Baptist could only
hold five hundred and he never had a service that brought in
less than twice that many. People standing in the aisles and
out in the foyer, all of them to see him, the man with the silver tongue. Why build another church? the deacons' board
was saying. We can just add another service to take care of
the overflow. And just who was supposed to preach that service? He wasn't some kind of factory worker to whom they
could assign overtime.

Jealousy, that's all it was. Deacon Bennett, leading this
whole parade against him, was angry because he was fat, old,

and bald-headed while he, Moreland, had kept his looks. He prided himself on his physique that could easily belong to a man half his age. Add to that his full head of hair, which, while turning gray, only augmented his elegance and sophistication and his burnished copper skin, still smooth and supple, and we're talking a magnificent specimen of a man—oh, yeah—undeniably magnificent. Even without the attention of the church sisters—which was pronounced, and always had been—he had a mirror. And thanks to good eyesight—unlike that half-blind fool Bennett—he knew exactly what it showed: him, Moreland T. Woods, ready and waiting to jump into his destiny.

He calculated that he needed a church of at least two thousand to form the base for his bid for public office. He was willing to start off slow and just get elected to the community board, but after that, it was all the way to the mayor's mansion. Then he could truly serve his people—and all the people of the city—from that perch. But you don't begin to command that type of respect from a church of only five hundred seats—that's barely a step above a good storefront church. He was no bootleg preacher, not him, Mama Lou's big man. "What kinda talk this be, huh?" his grandmother used to say back in Jamaica when he was trying to explain away a bad grade at school. "You Mama Lou's big man, there's greatness waiting for yuh, reach out and grab it."

Mama Lou, her fingers stiff with arthritis, sewing into the wee hours of the day to keep him in good schools, had been both mother and father to him for as long as he could remember. His father remained unknown even after his mother died. "A good wash for bad rubbage," Mama Lou would say. "Yuh father never had more than two shilling to rub together and soon as he had three, he run like a field rabbit to God knows where—and probably don't care—him being so worthless." Mama Lou had her heart set on Moreland being a doctor or a lawyer. He wasn't sure what he wanted to become, but he knew one day he'd have to leave the island of Jamaica to find out.

The answer came to him one day when he was eighteen years old and passing by the sugar cane fields on his way to school. It was a clear morning with a warm breeze bringing the scent of hibiscus and gently stirring the birds of paradise that grew like weeds in the settlement. He heard the whoosh, whoosh of the tall grass in the cane fields and something in the sound of it made him stop for a moment and peer into the fields. Moreland . . . Moreland . . . he believed he heard the grass whispering . . . And at that moment a heavy wind arose and bent the swaying cane so that it seemed they were bowing down to him. Thousands in a congregation that filled each horizon in front of him calling him to come serve.

Moreland had never been particularly religious. The regular services with Mama Lou on Sunday in the Anglican church satisfied his conscience and kept Mama Lou's mouth still. It be seven days yuh have, huh—one of them can't go to God? What's this wicked thing I'm raising? And since the one service kept her quiet, he felt no need to join the junior choir or the ushers' board. It would be hard to make those meetings so early anyway since his Saturday nights were spent carousing with his friends—spending money on good rum and bad women was money well spent the way he saw it. So his relationship with God had been fairly casual until he heard the whispering in the cane fields that he must serve.

But like the prophets of old, Moreland did not accept his fate without a little bargaining with God. If he gave up wine, women, and song—or any derivation thereof—what kind of church would God give him in return? Start small, the whispering cane told him the next day as he stood at its edge waiting for a sign. Start small and I will help you build. But Moreland wanted to know *how* small? There was Anglican small on the island with two hundred seats that was large by their standards but infinitesimal compared to the cathedrals in London. Or there was Pentecostal small with its fifty seats just on the edge of the town near the banana groves. If he gave up wine and just kept women and song, would that increase the size of the congregation? And if push came to shove and he gave up song as well, would that make a sizeable difference, and if so, how much of a difference? Or if he gave up women too—a huge sacrifice that he could barely stand to think about—surely there was a bishop's cap waiting for him, even in the almost inaccessible Anglican church? You're starting to be a royal pain in the butt, he heard from the cane fields—where is your faith? Well, his faith was still in himself, where it had always been. And maybe that was the real answer, just trust in himself and God would take care of the minor details. With that in his back pocket, he got himself a visa and left Jamaica for the United States.

• • •

Moreland felt that if anything was possible, it could be done in America. There was room to grow there, unlike Jamaica that would hold his background—and his grandmother's humble life—against him as he charted his rise to the top. Moreland still wasn't sure to the top of what, but at least it would be a beginning. He put himself through college by working days in a shoe factory, stitching straps onto women's sandals, and attending classes in the evening. It took him eight years to get his degree; and as he bent over the huge stitching machine he knew this couldn't be what the Lord meant when He talked in the scriptures about "saving souls," so he kept his eye out for the church that was going to propel him into his destiny.

He visited dozens of them during those eight years, from the small to the large, and finally settled on the Baptist Church. He liked the range found just within that one church—from storefront to five thousand seats—because it meant unlimited possibility. Why couldn't he take a church to ten thousand seats? Or even millions if you were talking about television evangelism? There was a bottom in the Baptist Church, but there was definitely no top. And when he looked at the great men of his race—the Martin Luther Kings—all had come out of the Baptist Church to go on to a national spotlight. Was he as great as Martin Luther King? No, but with enough work he could get there. That's what Annette kept telling him: "You can get there, Moreland, and I'll be right by your side."

His wife, Annette, had been a godsend for him. He met

her in one of his evening classes at the college. A snippet of a woman but with an appetite as large and ambitious as his. And it was finally on her advice that they became regular members of Sinai Baptist. It's a church that needs a leader, she told him. It was never filled to more than half capacity; a five-hundred-seater that only brought in half that number, even on Easter and Christmas. The congregation was primarily black and working-class, pulled from a fifty-block radius that included Brewster Place, a people hungry for good news. And Moreland was to bring that news—not only with himself—but with his preaching.

It had come as a shock to Moreland that he could be so comfortable up at the altar. That he, in fact, enjoyed preaching. The man with the silver tongue. The man who could make heaven feel high and hell low. But above all, a man who could give them respite from lives that were overworked and underpaid; lives that no one seemed to care about except them and the Lord—and Reverend Woods, of course. And so they kept him in his fancy clothes, his fancy car, and his brick home as a thank you and, above all, as an act of love returned.

Deacon Bennett wasn't buying it, not for one smooth-talking minute. Moreland Woods didn't need a new church; he needed, what the kids were calling today, an attitude adjustment. The man actually saw himself as some kind of prophet, sent into their dark and tangled midst to bring them light. A bucket of hogwash. He was simply one of the many that Bennett had seen come—and go—in his church over the years. And it was *his* church. He felt a part of every inch of Sinai Baptist; as a carpenter, he had even helped to build it—laid the cornerstone of the foundation and kept at it with the others—brick by brick. It was a beautiful church: the stained glass along both its sides; the solid walnut panels; the marble encasing the entire lobby. No expense had been spared to get quality material for the church, no effort left undone to see that it was almost a perfect job.

Deacon Bennett had never understood the people who argued that building such an elaborate church was a waste of money that could be going out into the community to help fight poverty or drugs or a host of other concerns. He was well versed in the needs of the black community; he was born and raised on Brewster Place. And it was hard to get more needy than that. But if you're moving out into the community and asking people to come to God's House, then it should look like God's House. A people were only as good and as strong as the gods they served; and when his people looked at Sinai Baptist they saw a beautiful, solid, and everlasting God asking them to stand up and be worthy of His attention.

Bennett had grown up going to a storefront church just two blocks south of Brewster Place. His mother was Pentecostal and his father a marginal Baptist so it was his mother's religion that had the most influence on him as a child. Pentecostals believed in the adage, "Make a joyful noise unto the Lord." Their services were unrestrained, with clapping hands and even "dancing holy" in the aisles. A service never went by that some sister of the church didn't faint and fall out from the touch of the Holy Spirit. Wonderful drama for him as a child who grew up believing that, bottom line, the purpose of religion was to make you feel.

When the Pentecostals lost their lease and moved to the other side of town, Bennett was sixteen years old and decided to change to the Baptist church, which also had its drama but a sense of pomp and circumstance, which appealed to his need for order. The red-robed choir coming down the aisles, singing and clapping in time to the music. And he loved seeing the ushers, black men in their best suits and white gloves, standing at attention all along the sides of the church. Dignified, straight-backed black men. No matter what their jobs were in the outside community, or even if they had no present work, once inside the church these men became somebody, at the least, a child of God. And that's not bad work if you can get it, they used to joke at the deacons' meetings. More black men needed to be in the church, Deacon Bennett would argue at the monthly board meetings. Too often the church was seen as the province of women. He'd spent a good part of his career in the church trying to balance the membership by starting the Samaritan League, an outreach program to net whole families as new members. And then just last year they began a mentor program where each male member was responsible for bringing just one young man to the services on Sunday—a way of getting their toes wet, so to speak, until they found out that the church could be a place—and sometimes the only place—for a black man to exercise leadership and responsibility.

In all his years he never felt the desire to get his own self ordained as a minister. He was much more comfortable as chair of the board of trustees and the deacons' board. The power behind the throne was true power to him. It was the deacons who had to approve of any new changes within the church; they were the ones at the center of the strategy meetings for spending any monies that went out. And yes, the minister had a seat on that board, but only one seat and one vote.

And with the church now full to capacity—credit going to Woods for some of this—it was time to begin thinking of using funds to support the programs that reached beyond their own door. Not a larger church to fit the ego of this present minister, but larger contributions to a scholarship fund for some deserving college students; a community center with tutors for the younger children, a gym for the older ones—a refuge after school until evening when it was time for the parents—or parent—to come home from work. Deacon Bennett even visualized the church building or subsidizing low income housing for some of its members or the community at large. A ministry poised for action, for making a difference in the world and not just serving its own end.

And Moreland Woods would just have to take his ego and his plans for using Sinai Baptist as a political launching pad somewhere else. He couldn't preach two sermons on Sunday for the overflow crowd? Just who in the blazes did he think he was? A little more than hired help is all. And that business about being called from the cane fields was starting to wear thin. After knowing the man these twelve years, Bennett was pretty sure a hangover was the cause of his hearing any kind of voices; and if he saw anything moving in

those cane fields, it was probably somebody's husband coming after him with a machete.

Taking on Moreland Woods as their minister had been a
mistake. And Deacon Bennett was trying to assess how big a
mistake. Could they afford to lose him at this juncture?
When a minister left a church, a certain number of the
membership was sure to follow; but would enough follow
him to hurt the church? The man seemed to live a charmed
life; none of the allegations that had come down over the
years had been enough to take him down.

He was discreet with his womanizing, that was for sure.
And when the women were called before the deacons' board
they all denied the rumors that had been circulating. He could
understand the married women's staunch denials; but even the
unmarried ones had come in protecting Woods. Women
never ceased to surprise Bennett. Give them a man with a
handsome face and a certain style at the podium and they
started falling like dominoes, thinking they were seeing real
power. But it was he, and not Woods, who was at the center of
real power at Sinai Baptist. And whatever he did, he needed to
consider the effect upon his church. He wasn't going to let
anyone destroy that—silver tongue or no—because it was
where he lived; where he found his true worth and calling.

Moreland was dressing carefully for his meeting with the
deacons' board that evening. He didn't want to wear one of
his really good suits because that might remind them of how
much money he was making. Not that they didn't know,
since they appropriated the funds, but it would be difficult

to be humble sitting up there in a five-hundred-dollar suit. He finally settled on his dark blue pinstripe with a light blue shirt. Rummaging through his tie rack was one of the many times when he truly missed Annette. His late wife, God rest her soul, would have known instinctively which of the silk ties would be the best. Nothing too flashy but nothing too somber either—he didn't want the deacons' board to feel that he was defeated before he even made his case. With a sigh he settled on a dark blue tie but with a pearl stickpin to give just a modicum of flash, reminding himself once again that he needed a new wife. But he knew he'd never be that lucky twice in row. Annette had been perfect, if perfection were possible in any human being. A wife who understood exactly where he was going; who understood the late hours; and above all, who understood the other women. As long as he was discreet, she remained silent. And that silence was more effective than any arguments or screaming would have been. It weighed like a club that he used to beat up on himself, promising with all his heart that it would never happen again. And it never did—until it happened again.

Maybe he should just let sleeping dogs lie and go on the way he had for the last six years: accountable to no one but himself in his personal life. And regardless of what the deacons said, his personal life was his. But they'd been trying hard to get rid of him—he knew that—by dragging some hapless woman into their boardroom and trying to get her to impeach him. As long as he stayed single there was no chance of that: the married ones wouldn't talk, of course, and neither would the unmarried, hoping that they might be the next Mrs. Woods. He saw these brief affairs as just a fringe benefit of the job. He'd forced none of them; had even to run like lightning from some.

So what were the deacons always trying to impeach him for? Adultery? Fornication? All of the things they were probably guilty of themselves if someone bothered to dig around their lives as they dug around his. No, they had nothing on him. Absolutely nothing. These inquisitions they were always setting up were just more of the same harassment and disrespect that Deacon Bennett was cheerleading for. Sometimes he wished he could just slap him upside his bald head. Bennett hated—absolutely hated—that Moreland was so popular with the parishioners. They could build him that lousy church he was asking for; Sinai Baptist was rich—hundreds of thousands invested in stocks and bonds—richer than even the parishioners knew. And would it kill them to just start a special collection for a building fund? The people would give gladly if they were asked in the right way. And Moreland knew exactly how to get them fired up.

His people loved him, that much he knew, and he'd often toyed with the idea of leaving Sinai Baptist and taking the whole crowd with him. Maybe he would do just that—tell the deacons' board that he would find another church that respected his dedication and service since they obviously didn't. But in truth it would take another twelve years of his life to build up to what he had now, and that fat ass, bald-headed Bennett knew it too. No, they had him in a corner but he was going to come out fighting at this very meeting. He was sick and tired of them holding him on such a short leash.

• • •

Deacon Bennett came especially early to the church to set up the boardroom for their meeting with Reverend Woods. As always, he felt a sense of calm when surrounded by the beauty and quiet within the church. He put notepads and pencils at each of the eight seats around the long mahogany table. A fresh flower arrangement was in the middle of the table; later it would go out to help adorn the altar so there would be no waste. He then made sure there was a fresh batch of coffee for the urn in the corner of the room and enough glasses for the bottles of water that he arranged around the floral centerpiece.

All was in order and now he just had to wait for his nephew to show up. He hoped the boy wasn't going to be late; he told him he had to be there by seven-thirty at the latest because the meeting would start promptly at eight. He was just about to recheck the coat closet again when he heard the bell to the side door. Terrific. It was Seymour.

His nephew was twenty-two and a struggling actor. Well, tonight he would get a chance to practice his skills. Bennett hid the boy in the coat closet and gave him his props: a straw broom and the round cylinder from an empty roll of paper towels. Remember, Bennett said, when I cough twice you go into action. Take the broom and sweep it lightly across the door. Then use the cylinder like a microphone and speak through it—it'll muffle your voice, okay? And don't worry about the other deacons; he'd already told them what was going down. They would have a little fun with Woods tonight.

The other deacons were all assembled by eight o'clock and waiting for Woods. He knew the man was going to be late—

his way of trying to prove that he and not the board was in control. But none of them showed a shred of impatience when he finally glided into the room half an hour late. Bennett had to hand it to him: he was smooth. The kind of man you might even want for your daughter until you looked under the surface and saw little but a total egomaniac.

After listening to the reading of the minutes from the last meeting and a list of the agenda for that night, Woods went immediately on the offensive. He had his arguments all laid out for why they needed a larger church. It wasn't for himself, of course, but only for the good of the congregation. And as he kept going on and on, it slowly turned to subtle threats. And on the wild chance that a new church might do him some good, didn't he deserve it? Hadn't he worked his fingers to the bone for Sinai Baptist these last twelve years? And if they didn't appreciate him, maybe, just maybe there might be another church that would. Even if he had to start it himself.

"Are you threatening us, Reverend Woods?" one of the deacons asked.

"Never. But I think it's time for us to lay all our cards on the table. Just why can't we build a new church?"

"I'll give you three reasons," Deacon Bennett said. "Money. Money. Money."

And then Bennett coughed twice. *Swish* . . . *Swish* . . . the strange sound seemed to be coming out of the walls.

"Deacon Bennett, you know as well as I do that Sinai has the money to begin laying a new foundation tomorrow if a majority at this table agrees. And besides . . ."

Swish . . . Swish . . . Woods stopped mid-sentence and frowned. "You hear something strange around here?"

He looked into seven blank faces. Nobody had heard a thing.

"I coulda sworn I just heard . . ."

Swish . . . Swish . . . More-land . . . More-land . . .

"Come on, what's going on here?" Woods said.

"Are you all right, Reverend Woods?" Deacon Bennett's face showed nothing but concern as he balled his fists up under the conference table trying to keep himself from laughing. The other men were brilliant—absolutely brilliant—as everyone kept a straight face.

"Reverend Woods," said another of the deacons, "would you like to rest for a while?"

"I don't need to rest. I just need to know what in the hell . . ."

Swish . . . Swish . . . More-land . . . More-land . . .

"Come on now, you had to hear that."

"Hear what?" Deacon Bennett asked.

"Somebody's calling my name, damn it!"

"Like in the cane fields?" Deacon Bennett asked again.

"Maybe it's only meant for you to hear," another deacon said. "You know, like with the prophets. Maybe it's the Lord."

Bennett almost lost it then—almost—but it was soon going to be a losing battle.

Swish . . . Swish . . . More-land . . . More-land . . .

"What's the Lord saying?" Bennett asked.

More-land . . . More-land . . . You ain't getting no new church, sucker, so take that—

And the room went wild. The deacons were all laughing so hard they were choking. Deacon Bennett laughed until he cried, his head bent over his arms on the conference table.

"You were looking kinda scared there, Woods, for a man who's used to talking with God," one of the deacons said.

Reverend Woods sat there like a stone—outraged.

"Come on, Woods, can't you take a joke?" Bennett said before calling his nephew out of the closet.

"The Lord's work is never a joke to me—never," Woods said. "None of you should have the nerve to be sitting in judgment of me and my life when this is how you carry on."

"Don't get all pompous on us," Bennett said, "it was just a joke. But you're right, there is serious business here at hand . . ." And Bennett lost it again, laughing and pulling a handkerchief out of his pocket to wipe his eyes.

"I'm gonna get you for this," Woods said. "You're all gonna be sorry you messed with me."

"Man, you take yourself too serious," Deacon Bennett said. "Lighten up a little. Now, about what you're really here for. We've heard your arguments for a new church and the board will take it all under advisement. We're going to put it to a vote and by our next meeting we'll have an answer for you. Is that satisfactory, Reverend Woods?"

"No, it's not," he said. "According to our bylaws I can call for a full referendum on this matter. Let the entire congregation vote."

"You don't want to do that," Bennett said. "You'll lose."

"I'll take my chances."

Woods got up from his seat, straightened his tie, and left without another word. The slamming door reverberated through the silent room.

Reverend Woods called for a full referendum to take place no later than two months from that July. Each member was entitled to one vote and the majority wins.

His battle for the heart and mind of Sinai Baptist was tireless and vicious. He used his pulpit to make his case, giving sermon after sermon about wolves in sheep's clothing; about a workman being worthy of his wages; and finally falling back upon his favorite J: Jesus Christ and all the hardships good shepherds must endure to bring light and salvation to an ungrateful people—people who went so far as to lie in order to have him crucified. They were magnificent sermons, full of fire, and everyone in the congregation knew he was targeting the deacons' board. But while Woods was up in his pulpit, sweating and straining; pounding the wood with one hand and raising the other to God, he knew that Deacon Bennett was very quietly spreading the rumor that if Sinai Baptist voted for a new church, it would bankrupt the congregation.

A rumor can spread like wildfire; it's more powerful than the truth, which just sits there, because it feeds on itself, growing larger with each passing day. A few choice words from Bennett and then he could just lie back and watch his rumor move from the plausible: Sinai Baptist couldn't afford a larger building without bankruptcy; to the ludicrous: Reverend Woods was being paid by the trustees of Mercy Baptist, their sister church, to split the congregation and cause the demise of Sinai Baptist. No, Woods couldn't fight rumors with the truth; he had to fight fire with fire.

Sister Louise was a godsend. She came to him nineteen, pregnant, and scared. No, she didn't know who the father was, but it had to be one of the two men she'd gone to bed with earlier in the year. And she didn't want any trouble, because one of them was on the deacons' board. Woods could have yelled "hallelujah" right then and there. He wanted to dance a jig. He wanted to kiss this wayward child who'd just given him a new church. But he managed to remain calm as he took her through the rest of the ritual. No, he didn't want to know the name of the man on the deacons' board; God knew and that's all that mattered. Was she repentant? Yes, she was. Well, good, because the Lord would find a way in His heart to forgive. He explained to her that this coming Sunday he would have to call her to the mourners' bench, where she would sit with the other members who were asking God—and the church—for forgiveness. You go to the mourners' bench with a troubled and dark heart, he told her, but you arise from it pure as the driven snow.

The Right Reverend Moreland T. Woods could hardly wait. This would be the mother of all Sundays. He rehearsed over and over in his mind exactly how he was going to choreograph the beginning of the end for the deacons' board. As usual his sermon would be taken from the book of Luke with the parable of the prodigal son; all those on the

mourners' bench having been returned now to their heav-
enly Father's house and carrying His forgiveness and grace.
But a little extra was in order with Sister Louise—her part-
ner in sin was still among them and he would call for that
man to come down to the mourners' bench, to save God's
wrath from descending on all the church.

Well, he called for that man at the end of his sermon and,
as expected, no one came. Sister Louise sat with her head
down, wiping tears from her eyes. Woods went and stood
before the pews reserved for the deacons' board.

"The Lord is asking again," he said. "Who will be man
enough to come and sit beside our sister? God already
knows your heart. It is not for man to judge—but Him.
Come, and sit beside our sister."

No one on the deacons' board moved a muscle or batted
an eye.

"I said, the Lord is asking once again—who will sit beside
our sister? Do you want her to call out the name that God
already knows? A dark and deceitful heart will not enter the
doors of heaven."

The congregation began to whisper and a few leaned over
in their seats to get a look at the faces on the deacons' board.
Woods went back to his pulpit, satisfied with his performance. All he needed was that whisper, because it was on its
way to growing into a roar. And that roar would become a
wave of anger against the faceless man without the guts to ask
God—and the church—for repentance. And Woods was going to ride that wave until it washed him ashore at the steps of
his new church. That one man was the rotten apple that

would spoil whatever influence Deacon Bennett was wielding. With no one man to chastise, the congregation would chastise them all. They would vote him that new church.

Woods looked into Bennett's eyes and, surprisingly, he caught a flicker of admiration. One good warrior to another.

A year later the day was cloudy and chill when a handful of parishioners assembled to witness the ceremony for laying the cornerstone of a new Sinai Baptist. Deacon Bennett officiated by digging the first shovel of dirt and then handing the shovel on to Reverend Woods. Woods dug his shovelful and another for good measure. To hear Bennett's benediction you would have thought that the entire idea belonged to the deacons' board and the board alone. Bennett lived by the old adage: If you can't beat 'em, build 'em a church. You retreat to fight another day, he thought. And fight he would to keep the congregation from splitting. It had almost come to that last year and so the deacons' board had backed off. He hadn't lost the war, just this one battle.

"I guess we'll be calling you Councilman Woods soon," Bennett said.

"If the Lord wills it," Woods responded. "But I know I can look forward to your personal support and the support of my church."

"Oh, I'll be there," Bennett responded. "Me and the Lord. Every step of the way."

C.C. Baker

Have a seat, C.C, this won't take long.

I'm not saying a motherfucking thing until I get a lawyer.

No one's accused you of anything; Detective Price and I just want to have a little chat.

So why the fucking cameras?

Insurance. Later we might disagree on how you were treated. But the video never lies. What goes down here is on the straight and narrow.

Good. So give me a straight fucking lawyer.

Do you wanna be charged? It can be arranged.

I ain't done nothing.

So talk to us.

Fuck you.

He moves in a world where he doesn't need more than a fifty-word vocabulary. And half of that fifty is some variation of the word, fuck. It becomes noun, adjective, adverb, and verb. And in his nine-teen years he's never taken a trip out of the city. But he knows the streets around Brewster Place like the back of his hand. And in those thirty square blocks he has a place to sleep; finds food to eat; beer to drink; and a movie theater to handle his dreams. He makes his money from petty hustling: snatching a bag or two; running mes-sages between a lady and her pimp; dropping off dime bags for mid-level drug dealers. But he dreams of so much more; he dreams of escape. He doesn't want to be a punk all his life. And the way out of the ghetto is to be taken on by Beetle Royal—a top-level dealer who keeps his business tight and his lieutenants in good cars and good clothes. How could it occur to him that there might be a better way? Where does he get to being smart and ambitious with a ninth-grade education—a poor ninth-grade education—leaving him with enough ability to count his money at the end of the day and to read a TV Guide so he knows when the basketball games are on? You're heading straight for the graveyard or the jail, his father says. And C.C. honestly doesn't care as long as the ride to either is smooth and top-shelf.

See, you got a attitude problem, C.C. Nobody's talking that way to you. We show you respect—show us some.

You wanna nail me and you know it.

Nail you for what?

Everything. Anything. You're cops.

Just trying to do a job. Underpaid and overworked. So help us out a little.

What's in it for me?

Answer us straight—you walk. Try to get fancy, we book

you, and then you'll really need that lawyer you kept screaming about. What do you know about Hakim?

Nothing.

He was your brother.

That mean I carried him on my back?

He's dead, C.C.

So why ain't you looking for the fuckers who did it?

We're trying.

And he wasn't my real brother—he was a stepbrother.

Shame the way they shot him up. Straight to the face.

Yeah, my old man's taking it real bad.

You got any clues about who coulda done it?

It's close to Christmas—try Santa Claus.

He's only twelve years old when his mother and father stop trying. They can't keep him in school and off the streets. His father came back from Vietnam with one leg and three of his fingers blown off. A bitter man, he keeps his Purple Heart framed and on the living room wall: to remind him that this country ain't worth shit as he fights the V.A. to raise his disability pension. His mother works full-time to keep them off welfare. But there are six children in this home—two his father brought from another marriage—and only so much energy to go around. They lost the oldest boy, Hakim, to the streets and he hasn't been home in three years. So they tried harder with C.C. but the streets call to him as well with the promise of everything he sees missing in his father's life: money, power, and respect.

You got a sense of humor. We like that. Tell us about Hakim—he had a sense of humor too?

A laugh a minute.

Nice guy like that—who'd wanna take him out?

I ain't got no idea.

He was fronting for Tito. You know that.

News to me.

Well, it's not news for anybody else on the street. And we figure him being your brother . . .

Stepbrother.

Whatever. Family.

You see me sitting here—this is my fucking family. I owe nobody nothing.

He runs with a gang but when he looks in the mirror he sees the only face he can trust. Moving as a pack they roam the streets, loving the look of fear in the eyes of pedestrians who move quickly out of their way—some even stepping into the gutter—as they claim more than their share of the sidewalks. They're bad and they know it. Bad and they love it. Bad and always looking for a way to prove it. C.C. knows it's a punk move to keep running with the others. He needs a way to set himself apart so he can be noticed. His big break comes when one of Royal's lieutenants gives him a kilo to "mule" on the other side of town. He does it fast and with no sweat, chancing that the Narcs might pick him up just for coming out that building. They don't. So for six months he carries for Royal's lieutenant, knowing enough to hide the stuff in his parents' home and wait when the Narcs are laying heat on that side of town.

His parents stopped asking him long ago where he was going and why. He lies about the money he's bringing into the house—and they pretend to believe the lies because they need the help. It is then that he loses the last bit of respect he has for his father. Cripple-ass motherfucker—any fool knows that McDonald's doesn't pay you in hundred-dollar bills. Better to say, Son, I know you're dealing and thanks for the help. Or Son, I know you're dealing and keep that shit out of my house. But it's only some punk-ass, jive-ass who can't look you in the face like a man and face the truth. If anything, C.C. never lies to himself. He wouldn't last a month on the streets if he did. No make-believe, no damn fairy tales: He is dealing and proud of it. And wants his old man to be proud of it too.

Tell us what you know about Royal.

Nothing. Never heard of him.

Look, here's the deal, C.C. You don't insult our intelligence—and we don't insult yours. Anybody over three years old on Brewster Place knows about Royal. Hometown boy makes good. Buying turkeys for Thanksgiving. Candy for Christmas. A real upright citizen. Makes us all proud to be black.

I never got no turkey.

That why you angry with him?

How can I be mad with somebody I don't even know.

Never worked for him?

No.

There is no conscience in the streets. And there is only one golden rule: Do unto others, hard, fast, and thorough so the fuckers think twice before doing it back to you. The most important thing in any man's life is self-respect. And how in the hell can you have self-respect if you're sniveling and crying over every loser who gets dumped on and taken out? Some people deserve what they get by be-ing stupid. And it's the stupidest thing in the world to think about messing over something that belongs to Royal. He is The Man. The Mack. And when The Man calls—as he does for C.C.—you go with fear and trembling in your heart; praying, as you would with any god, that you be found worthy to serve.

We think Royal might be behind your brother's death.

I ain't got a clue.

You know, with the turf war going on now with Tito.

Not a clue.

C.C., if you keep lying about this little shit, how we gonna believe you when it comes to the real questions?

Like what?

Like why Royal used you to set up Hakim. He has other lieutenants.

Man, you're outta your fucking mind. I ain't killed no-body.

We said, set up—we didn't say, kill.

It's what you meant.

Now you're reading our minds? A smart guy like you must be worth a fortune to Royal.

I don't know no Royal.

And you don't run errands for him?

I ain't nobody's punk—get that?

The Man does not disappoint. His office. His suit. His haircut. His manicure. All well above top-shelf. There is nothing in that room that does not say elegant and good taste. C.C. is invited to take a seat on a couch with leather so smooth and soft it's like sitting in the lap of a woman. Dim lights hang over the oil paintings on the wall: there is even a Picasso among them. African masks and two-foot African sculptures round out the art in this place. And off in the corners sitting quietly with their Uzis are two dark archangels in charge of keeping peace in this heaven. Royal speaks softly and moves his brown delicate hands when he talks as if conducting a small ensemble. He will tap one finger against another or jab the air to make his points. He is looking for a new junior lieutenant, someone to go into training for helping to control the east side of his territory. He's been keeping tabs on C.C. for quite a while and likes what he sees. The young man is smart and ambitious, but the question remains—could he also be loyal?

What did Royal promise you, C.C.? That you'd be a lieutenant?

I think you guys must be sniffing something—

Let me tell you what we think, C.C., and you tell us if we're hot or cold. We think Royal had someone take out Hakim as a test of loyalty. Royal likes 'em loyal—if you'll excuse the poetry. So here we have somebody—who you don't know—offing your brother for a piece of shit like Royal—who you also don't know. Your brother worked for Tito—another piece of shit—who you've never heard of. And Hakim's murder was a warning that if Tito stepped his Puerto Rican ass over into Royal's territory, it's gonna be all-out war. And all of this is news to you 'cause you been busy singing in the choir on Sunday. We got it about right, brother man?

Just 'cause you cops are both black don't make you my brother.

He stands at the corner with a .45 Magnum hid under his down jacket. His heart is beating so loudly he can hear it drumming in his ears. A raw wind blows and it seems to fill his head as he spits to take the taste of brass from his mouth. The fucker deserves it. Nobody messes with Royal—he's The Man. And Hakim is just another punk that needs to be taught a lesson. Long ago the street washed away any memories that might make this job impossible: Hakim piling up the gifts he'd bought under the Christmas tree— the one year everybody in the family got what they wanted. Nintendos and bicycles; new TVs and VCRs. Just pocket change, Hakim said to him with a wink. Hakim sharing his first joint with C.C. and laughing when the smoke chokes him. No, little brother—inhale and hold. Hakim, his arms around his shoulder, warning him never to take nothing stronger than a reefer. This shit we sell is for scum and losers—and you never wanna be a loser, a punk-ass.

What makes a brother, C.C. What did Hakim do so that he was no longer your brother? So you would help stamp him out as if he was a lousy cockroach?

Man, this ain't nothing but a fucking setup. I can smell a setup a mile away. Book me and let me call a goddamned lawyer.

There you go, talking lawyer when we're just trying to get a few things cleared up.

Not another fucking word without a lawyer.

When he finally sees Hakim, he tells himself that he's trembling from the cold—he'd been at that corner an hour. And his hands are turning numb even with the thick gloves. Yo, Hakim. And when he gets closer, C.C. pulls the Magnum from under his coat. Hakim starts to laugh, This a joke, Little Brother, what's up? For the first time in his life, C.C. begins to pray. Please, God, let me do this right. Give me a chance—for once—to be a real winner.

We're gonna do you a favor, C.C. We're gonna book you and get you off the streets.

He aims for the face so he won't have to see his brother's eyes as he dies. He does as instructed: he throws the gun by the body and runs off. The punk-ass deserved it. C.C. runs and he runs and he runs . . .

I'll be out with one phone call.

Who you gonna call, C.C.? Tito? Royal? All those people you don't know.

Read me my rights so I can get the fuck out of here.

What about Hakim's rights, C.C.? Didn't he have a right to live?

. . . C.C. runs and runs until he's crying from the cold wind whipping his face as he thanks God for giving him the courage to do it. The courage to be a man.

ABSHU

Fall is the best time of the year for me, even though you only know that it's come on this street because the children start wearing sweaters and the adults move into light jackets. I tell myself to count my blessings that there ain't any leaves to sweep up and burn. We get just a chilly edge to the air with the complaints rolling in that there ain't enough heat being sent up. Company policy is that I keep the furnace fired up from the middle of October till the middle of May—regardless of the weather. But I use my own judgment and when we get an Indian summer, like this year, I may not send up heat until we're well into November. But some folks are so senseless they'll start yelling and waving their leases stating that they're entitled to heat in October even though it's not needed. I could have this job for a hundred years and I'll still never understand people. Not that I think I wanna understand them. I've seen it all: the good, the bad, and the ugly. Even though the bad and the ugly are out there loud and hard to miss, maybe we don't concentrate enough on the good because they're so few.

And speaking of the good, I've watched Cliff Jackson grow up from a skinny little kid to the fine man that he is today. I don't much understand why he changed his name to Abshu, but some of them are doing that today, talking about it makes them feel closer to Africa and our beginnings. For me, I figure that one name is the same as the next, it's what a man's done with his life that counts regardless of what name he's done it under. But if it makes him feel better to be called Abshu, I call him Abshu. It don't make me no never mind; and when I think about it, my full name is Benjamin but I've been called Ben all my life and it's worked just as good. I don't think things woulda turned out any different for me if I'd gone by Benjamin all my life. But I'm the past, and these young kids like Cliff Jackson are the future. And if there were more like him, I could rest a little easier about where we're gonna end up as a people.

Clifford Montgomery Jackson was sitting down with his second cup of coffee and a notepad on which he was plotting the assassination of the Reverend Moreland Woods.

He did this religiously each day with the same regularity as jogging or taking a full run through the park. He entertained himself this morning trying to calculate the number of years they would give him in jail. He figured that since there wasn't a spot on his record, not even a recent parking ticket, the most he'd come out with was twenty-five to life. And with a good lawyer it would probably get knocked down to under twelve. After all, it was only going to be justifiable homicide—very justifiable. The man was ripe for killing, needed killing, in light of his performance at the city council meeting in the vote about Brewster Place.

Woods had run for office, begging them for support to be the first black member of the city council. It was to be his mission to act as their eyes and ears—their voice on issues affecting the black community. They believed him and worked like demons to get him elected on one of the smallest margins in the city's history, but still enough to win him a seat. And no sooner did he take off his hat and jacket than he betrayed them. The wall was coming down and Brewster Place was slated to be condemned and the whole area rebuilt as middle-income housing—condos as a matter of fact. Maybe it wouldn't have hurt as much if it had been the twentieth issue the council was voting on or even the seventh. But it was the first vote and Woods decided the tiebreaker. His vote for demolition could only be taken as an "up yours" to the people who had put him on the council. And he wouldn't have to worry about their help again, would he? The homeless don't vote, and neither do people who move out of town. And the city council knew that was the fate for most of the people on Brewster Place—thanks to Moreland T. Woods.

Clifford Jackson, or Abshu, as he preferred to be known in the streets, had committed himself several years ago to use his talents as a playwright to broaden the horizons for the young, gifted, and black—which was how he saw every child milling around that dark street. As head of the community center he went after every existing grant on the city and state level to bring them puppet shows with the message to avoid drugs and stay in school; and plays in the park such as actors rapping their way through Shakespeare's *A Midsummer Night's Dream*. Abshu believed there was something in Shakespeare for everyone, even the young of Brewster

Place, and if he broadened their horizons just a little bit, there might be enough room for some of them to slip through and see what the world had waiting. No, it would not be a perfect world, but definitely one with more room than they had now.

The kids who hung around the community center liked Abshu, because he never preached and it was clear that when they spoke he listened; so he could zero in on the kid who had a real problem. It might be an offhand remark while shooting a game of pool or a one-on-one out on the basketball court, but he had a way of making them feel special with just a word or two. And if they showed up with bruises on their faces or arms, like Nancy did one day, he wasn't going to stop until he found out what happened. He wasn't so quick to call the authorities because he knew the hell that foster care could be; but he would go to their homes and talk to their parents, trying to see if there was something the family could do to pull things back together.

Abshu wished that his own family could have stayed together. There were four of them who ended up in foster care: him, two younger sisters, and a baby brother. He understood why his mother did what she did, but he couldn't help wondering if there might have been a better way. Yes, his father was a brutal man; a man who brought every insult, every failed job application, back to their home at night. And what he couldn't say—or wouldn't say—to the outside world, he said to Abshu's mother with his fists. Anything could set him off: a burned pot of rice, a television left on with no one watching, toys scattered on the living-room floor—anything. Abshu remembers being eight years old, lying in bed at night and listening to his mother's muted cries through his own tears and promising himself that as soon as he was grown, he was going to take her away from that—take all of them away. And the sick thing about it was that his father did those beatings cold sober. How could a man who was stone sober break a woman's arm? When he was drunk was the time for him to apologize, to beg her for another chance, which somehow she managed to give him. And so you sit at the dinner table in a world where nothing is sane and predictable, hearing his key turn the lock on the door, and praying that your father will be drunk that night.

When the beatings began on the children his mother decided it was enough. "Maybe I ain't much," she said. "No education. No job. But you children are all I have. He beats me is one thing; but not my kids." She was packing their things for them to leave when the Child Protection Agency came to the house. A teacher had reported the bruises on the side of his sister's face. They were all put in foster care, broken up and sent to different homes. His mother had tried to get them placed together, but it was hard enough to find a decent family to take one child, no less the four of them. "It's just until I get myself together," his mother said. "Till I get me a job and see my way clear."

Abshu was put into a home that already had two other boys from foster care. The Masons lived in a small wooden bungalow right on the edge of Linden Hills. And Mother Mason insisted that they tell anybody who asked that they actually lived *in* Linden Hills, a more prestigious address than Summit Place. It was a home that was kept immaculate. Plastic covers on the living-room furniture, and plastic flowers adorning the tables in every room of the house, even the boys' bedroom. Shoes came off in the foyer before entering and socks came off for the laundry as soon as they hit their bedrooms. "Dirty feet—stink, stink." Mother Mason always used baby talk. A tiny woman in her fifties who twittered like a bird. She sat in sharp contrast to Father Mason, a big hulking man who rarely spoke. And the boys were required to address them as they addressed each other— Mother Mason and Father Mason.

But what he remembered most about the Masons was that it seemed there was never quite enough to eat. She sent them to school with a lunch of exactly one and a half sandwiches—white bread spread with margarine and sprinkled with sugar—and half an apple. And if they complained of hunger before Father Mason came home they'd get the other half of the apple with a glass of milk. "No more until supper," she would twitter. "Don't be a piggy-piggy." No one ate in this house at dinnertime until Father Mason did, even if he was working a few hours overtime. When he came in, they had to wait for him to take the bath that Mother Mason had run for him in the tub, to change into a shirt and pants from his work overalls, and finally to sit at the table with a long blessing over the food. To Abshu it seemed like the blessing went on for days as his stomach grumbled. And even then Father Mason was to be served first. It seemed as if she had a calculator in her head because there were never any leftovers for a second helping. If she cooked a chicken it was divided into six servings: two for Father Mason and one piece each for the rest of them. Abshu learned to chew even the bones to tide himself over until breakfast: bacon and eggs for Father Mason, a small bowl of cereal for everyone else. Asking for seconds was to be met with suspicion from Mother Mason—"Shame. Shame. Are you trying to say we mistreat you here? Don't be a piggy-piggy."

When Abshu dreamed of leaving—which was every day—he had his own apartment with a refrigerator overflowing with food that he gorged himself with day and night. The Masons weren't mean people; he knew he could have ended up with a lot worse. Bobby, one of the other foster boys in their house, was now on his third foster home. And he had stories that made Abshu's father seem like a saint. His mother wrote to him often and he didn't tell her or his social worker that he was hungry much of the time; he simply stole candy bars from the corner grocery. There were no allowances given in the Mason home. "Why do you need money?" Mother Mason asked. "Don't we already give you everything you need?"

He lived with these people for nine years, won a scholarship to the local college, and moved out to support himself through school by working in a doughnut shop. He put on over thirty pounds in one year and he was still a little underweight for his size. By this time his mother was ready to take her children back home, but he decided that since he was already out on his own he would stay there. One less mouth for her to worry about feeding. And after he graduated with his degree in social work, he might even be able to give her a little money to help her along.

One thing he did thank the Masons for was keeping him out of gangs. There was a strict curfew in their home that was rigidly observed. And church was mandatory if you believed in God or not. "When you're out on your own," Father Mason always said, "you can do whatever you want, but in my home you do as I say." No, they weren't mean people, but they were stingy—stingy with their food and with their affection. Existing that way all the time, on the edge of hunger, on the edge of kindness, gave Abshu an appreciation for a life fully lived. Do whatever job makes you happy, regardless of the cost; and fill your home with love. Well, his home became the community center right around the corner from Brewster Place and the job that made him most fulfilled was working with young kids. Returning to the scene of the crime was how he joked with himself about it. Although his own father was long gone and his mother was living on the other side of town, he always thought of Brewster Place as his first—and only—home.

The kids who hung out at the community center weren't all lost yet. They wanted to make use of the tutors for their homework; and they wanted a safe place to hang. His motto was: Lose no child to the streets. And on occasion when that happened, he went home to cry. But he never let his emotions show at work. To the kids he was just a big, quiet kind of dude who didn't go looking for trouble, but he wouldn't run from it either. He was always challenged by a new set of boys who showed up at the center. He made it real clear to them that this was his territory—his rules—and if they needed to flex their muscles, they were welcome to try. And he showed many that just because he was kind, it didn't mean he was weak. Not a few had been lifted up by the collar and thrown bodily out of the door. And when they returned—if they returned—they respected him. And the ones who didn't return, just didn't return: there had to be rules someplace in their world, some kind of discipline. And if they understood that, then he worked with them, long and hard, to let them see that they could make a difference in their own lives. They didn't need guns and they didn't need mouths like sewers to get respect.

Little Sammy and his friends were always getting beat up by a crowd of larger boys until Abshu showed him how he could fight back with nothing but his mouth and his wits. And it didn't have to be a string of filth—fuck this; fuck that; and the infamous fuck you. Abshu spent three weeks with the boys teaching them to curse like Shakespeare did. It'll work wonders for you, he tried to convince the boys. They won't know what to do with you, and if all else fails, then you fight—but not before. Abshu's method was put to the test when Sammy and two friends were at the pool table. Billy and his crowd didn't want to wait their turn and were trying to push the smaller boys away.

"Just get the hell out of here, punks," Billy said. But Sammy wasn't willing to give up his turn. "You want me to take that cue stick," Billy said, "and jam it up your . . ."

"You drone," Sammy said.

"What'd you just call me?"

"You drudge, you clog," Sammy went on. "You unbaked and doughy youth."

"Man, what language you talking? Are you bugging out?"

"You tyrant," one of Sammy's friends piped up. "You carcass fit for hounds."

"Yeah," another of Sammy's friends said, "you ain't getting our turn, you base wretch, you unspeaking sot—you pigeon liver."

Billy stood there as confused as he would have been if Sammy and his friends had slammed him upside the head.

"What in the hell they talking about? Someone tell me what in the hell is going on?"

"We said, it's our turn at the pool table, you devil incarnate, you child of hell—you foolish cur."

"Yeah, thou lump of foul deformity . . ."

"A pox on your throats . . ."

"Something's happening here." Billy looked at his homeboys for support and saw them as confused as he was. "Tell me, what's happening here?"

"They need their asses kicked," one of Billy's crowd said, "that's all."

But Sammy held on to the cue stick: "Oh, wretched fool. Consumption catch thee. Go shake your ears."

"I think he's crazy," Billy said. "Man, let's just leave him alone—he's crazy."

"This is the silliest stuff that ever I heard," Sammy said.

"I'm telling you," Billy said, "he's crazy. And it's probably catching. Let's just get the hell out of here."

But Sammy's crowd wasn't through yet—they had the enemy planning a retreat and they recited at their turned backs: "Were I like thee, I'd throw away myself."

"More of your conversation would affect my brain."

And then the small boys spoke together in unison as the larger ones hit the door: "You starvelling, you eel-skin, you dried neat's tongue, you bull's-pizzle, you stock-fish—Oh for breath to utter what is like thee!—you tailor's yard, you sheath, you bow-case, you vile standing *tuck!*"

With the enemy in total rout, they gave themselves high fives. And Abshu, who had intentionally turned his back on the whole drama, gave silent thanks that, unlike in rehearsal, none of the boys slipped up and ended the Shakespearean cursing by calling their opponent a vile standing *fuck.* He was so proud of them he could have shouted. These were the moments that weighed in against the heartbreaking aspects of his job.

And it was also moments like these that only reinforced the fact that Moreland Woods needed killing. Someone should put him out of his misery, because how could he not be miserable knowing that kids like Sammy were going to be uprooted soon and sent out into that cycle of despair that comes with being homeless? But then again maybe he wasn't miserable; maybe he felt just fine knowing that he had ingratiated himself to at least half of the city councilmen with his very first vote. Maybe he knew that his lies about finding the displaced families a new home were just that—lies—and he honestly didn't give a damn? No tossing and turning at night; no second thoughts; no remorse. Maybe he was just what he appeared to be: a heartless son of a bitch who wanted to get to the top without thinking about the people he had to step on? Yeah, just maybe Woods was the consummate politician in the making—take no prisoners and make sure the reporter spells your name right.

Abshu was sitting in a coffee shop across from City Hall, trying to plan new strategies since Woods refused to make any more appointments with him. At first Abshu followed the law to the letter in trying to lobby Woods and the other councilmen he'd voted with to destroy Brewster Place. With the other councilmen it was the usual runaround, the usual I understand your concerns, my heart is with you but my hands are tied type of bullshit. But with Woods it was different: he knew that Abshu knew he had consciously betrayed the trust the community put in him and there was no way to wiggle out of that first vote without more lies that insulted Abshu's intelligence. In a sort of twisted way his refusing to take a meeting with Abshu was a compliment: I know you're too smart for the standard crap I hand out, so there's nothing to be accomplished by a meeting. He could have given more promises, but Abshu would've laughed in his face; and not even leave him with the illusion that he was believed.

That's often what keeps politicians thinking of themselves as working for the common good—promises. Promises they can tell themselves they mean to make good—and some even try—until the harsh reality hits them with the fact that there's no way it can happen realistically. And so it's not their fault, is it? They wanted to do the right thing—wanted to fulfill those promises—until the reality of the political process hits them in the face. Abshu knew that Woods wasn't meeting with him because he couldn't look him in the eye and get what he needed for his own self-respect: a mutual agreement for them both to operate as if they believed that the next promises would not be broken; and the next, and the next . . .

Abshu looked down at what he'd been doodling on his pad. He had drawn a hangman with a rope and a scaffold. Hanging, yeah, he could see that for Woods. And tar and feathers. And a gunshot through the heart—no, not the heart because Woods didn't have one—go for the head. Poison was a good possibility except he wasn't letting Abshu anywhere near him lately. Maybe if he wrote Woods a letter, saying that he, Abshu, had seen the error of his ways and could they meet on some other matters than the demolition of Brewster Place? Invite him for dinner; no, he'd never accept the invitation; then a quick cup of coffee. And he could drop the poison in his coffee. He was down to running him over with a car when he heard his name called. Abshu looked up to see his friend, B.B. Rey, coming toward his table.

"Hey, man, I called you twice and you never heard me. What's up?"

"Nothing much. What're you doing here?"

"I've got a deposition to file over in the federal court."

B.B. looked down at Abshu's pad. "Oh, you're killing Woods again."

"Each time I do this, B.B., it becomes more of a reality."

"That's why you got me worried. There are other ways to

go about this, man, you could make him wish he was dead and then you save yourself all that prison time."

"How can I make him wish he was dead? He won't meet with me, and he's even stopped taking my calls. What's my next step, have you sue him?"

"No, get his attention."

"I'm all ears."

"You know the old joke, Abshu, about the man and his mule? A man has this stubborn mule who he's trying to move along and the animal won't budge. And so he's whipping the mule and whipping the mule to no avail. A traveler comes along the road and sees the man just laying into this mule with a strap and he says to the guy, 'Hey, that's no way to treat an animal. If you want the mule to cooperate you gotta treat him kind, treat him gentle.' And so the guy with the mule says, 'If you can do better, go right ahead.' So the traveler picks up a huge log that's laying by the road, hauls off and slams the mule with it right between the eyes. So the mule's wobbling on its legs and looking all cross-eyed. And the mule's owner says, 'Hey what's all this about? I thought you said, you gotta treat him kind, treat him gentle.' 'That's right,' the traveler replied, 'but you gotta get his attention first.'"

This gets a good laugh from Abshu. "You're a mess, B.B."

"In more ways than one."

B.B. Rey owed his name to his mother's love of the blues and jazz. She named him after B.B. King, giving him a lifetime of explaining that the two B's stood for nothing but two B's. His father was a Puerto Rican who retired from the post office when he was only fifty-five to now spend half his time big-game fishing in the Caribbean. And his mother, in his own words, never retired from being a certified nut. There wasn't a drop of Latino blood in her veins, she was more an American goulash with bits of Irish, a sprinkling of Scottish, a touch of German, and a whopping dose of French. None of which she felt made her more interesting than her husband who could claim at least one whole culture. She trained her children to say they were Colombian instead of Puerto Rican because to her that was a better class of Latino.

"Why not Cuban?" B.B. would ask her as he grew older. "They're big-time drug importers like the Colombian cartel. All the poor Puerto Ricans do is deal on the streets. And how do you think Papi feels knowing you want us to pretend we're Colombian?"

"I married for love," his mother said, "but I'm raising my children for success."

As family legend had it, she would stand over B.B.'s crib and whisper, lawyer, lawyer, you're going to be a lawyer. So, unlike other infants, when B.B. first spoke it wasn't "ma-ma" or "da-da" or any of that stuff. His first words were "litigate, litigate" which he took to mean "I'm hungry, bring me a bottle." But he quickly moved to the next stage of yelling "habeas corpus" when he wanted to be picked up and held or "objection, objection" when he wanted to say no.

Abshu often wondered how much of B.B.'s past was true and how much was just B.B. being B.B., who never considered flamboyance as one of the cardinal sins and practiced it often in his personal life as well as in court. A short, strapping fellow, he was the favorite of many judges, even those who threatened many times over the years to have him jailed for contempt. A civil rights lawyer, he was famous for giving his clients a passionate and thorough defense, something that people like them—or even the courts—were rarely used to. Once he even brought a goat in the courtroom although he was unsuccessful in having it sworn in as a witness.

"Your problem," B.B. told Abshu, "is an easy one. We find out Woods's weakness and we go for that."

"The man's a minister. Beyond being a heartless son of a bitch, I don't think he has many vices."

"Everybody's got a vice, Abshu; some little secret thing lying around in the closet at home. From what I've heard about Woods it's probably women. As a matter of fact, I can almost bet it's women."

"You would know about that—wouldn't you? You're awful lucky in that department."

"I stand accused."

B.B.'s success with women wasn't a matter of luck. He understood human nature and, above all, women. The way he saw it women always wanted to save a man from . . . something, anything. And the way he scored so highly on the first date—and definitely by the third—was by giving them that chance.

"I'm not gay," he would say, looking deeply into his date's eyes, "but sometimes I can feel that pull."

"Have you ever been with a man?" she'd ask.

"Never," he'd assure her. "But, you know, there is still that . . . pull."

"You just need a good woman," she'd say, "and things will be all right."

"I think I've found her," B.B. would say as he reached for her hand across the table. If she didn't squeeze back, he was in for more work. But if she squeezed back, he was home free.

For the more stubborn ones he would go into Plan B: he'd call her from a public phone booth on the corner from the notorious gay bar, the Purple Cock, and beg her to come down and get him before he walked through the door. He was feeling, he'd tell her, that awful . . . pull. This ploy worked on about ninety percent of the ones who hadn't let him score on the first date. And the final ten percent he gave up as the unfortunate few who would never experience a night in paradise with him.

"Yeah, I'm telling you," B.B. continued, "I'd lay you five-to-one that we can nail Woods by finding out exactly what goes between him and women."

"You're talking like kinky sex?"

"I'm talking any kind of sex—if we do it right. And I've just got a great idea. When does the city council meet again?"

"A week from Monday."

"That's pulling it a little close, but I think we can carry it off. How many actresses do you know?"

The day the city council met dawned clear and bright. It was one of those warm days of spring that felt more like summer. Many were inclined to toss their jackets and sweaters for shorts and T-shirts. There was a small demonstration going on outside City Hall since the council was slated to be debating the libraries' budget for the coming year. There was always some sort of demonstration when the council met, but that day was to bring the mother of all demonstrations straight inside to the public galleries. The council had been meeting for half an hour when the chanting began two blocks away. From the distance it sounded like the rumbling of thunder until it got close enough to be made out as wheels—the wheels on baby carriages. About fifty women, half of them with baby carriages and the others seeming to be in various stages of pregnancy, holding placards, formed a small army as they marched, double time, toward City Hall. They were a living United Nations: some brown, some black, some red—and even some white. Soon their chants could be heard even in the auditorium where the council was seated.

> *Moreland, Moreland*
> *Where's your shame?*
> *You left and didn't give*
> *My baby a name.*

As the women began to form a picket line in front of City Hall, they were joined by the library contingent, who knew a good thing when they saw it, and even a few male stragglers who took up some of the placards because they had nothing but time on their hands. B.B. and Abshu milled among these men. Their placards read: DADDY, GIVE ME A HOME; and MORELAND IS THE ONE . . . So when they finally marched into the council meeting, there were about a hundred people, ninety percent of them women. And among that ninety percent one or two of them might have actually been pregnant. WE WANT JUSTICE—NOT REVENGE read one placard. DADDY, WHEN ARE YOU COMING HOME? read another.

The chairman of the council was banging his gavel on the table: "Order, I want order in this place."

But these determined madonnas filled up the public gallery with their overstuffed bellies and their chanting. The members of the city council sat there stunned. Moreland Woods looked as if he'd stepped into a bad dream.

"Do you know these women?" the chairman asked Woods.

"I swear to you, I have never seen any of them in my life."

"So what's going on here?" asked the vice chair.

"They're lying," Woods said. "They're trying to destroy me."

"All of them?" The chairman looked at Woods. He was torn between horror and admiration for the man. "All of them?"

In spite of the gavel banging over and over again, the chanting continued from the gallery:

Blood tests, blood tests
We won't rest
Until we get a blood test.

"I'm calling for order in this room!" The chairman's face was close to beet red. "One more word and I'll have the marshals drag you out!"

"Yeah right," B.B. said to Abshu. "That'll look great on the evening news. Pregnant women and babies thrown bodily out of City Hall. We're home clear, Speedo."

"I coulda done Geraldo," one of the women yelled, "but I told 'em, No. I ain't going on TV; I want justice not revenge. And I still love you, Moreland."

"Yeah, we still love you," several others piped up.

> *But blood tests, blood tests*
> *We won't rest*
> *Until we get a blood test.*

Moreland Woods jumped up from his seat and pounded on the table. "I don't know *any* of you women. Why are you doing this?"

"You mean you don't know me?" A Latino woman, in her early twenties, with the largest belly in the crowd pushed herself up from her seat. She stood there with her hands on her hips and her stomach thrust forward, her face a study in indignation. "Here I am, the doctor telling me I'm carrying twins, and you don't know me? Well, good, I don't need you to take care of my babies. I'll take care of my own babies—you hear me—they need milk, I'll find 'em some milk; they need diapers, I'll get my own damn diapers. I'm just here for some justice, ya know? And when they're born don't come crawling around me

anymore, 'cause I'm naming 'em after you: Mother and
Fucker. So take that, Papi, and stuff it up your . . ."

"She's terrific," B.B. said to Abshu. "Where'd you find
her?"

"Yale."

Needless to say, there was no more business done by the
city council that day. Moreland Woods was asked to resign,
and although he was a fighter and could have asked for a
full hearing—let his accusers come to him one by one,
face-to-face—he didn't want to risk the outside possibility
that maybe one or two of the fifty was telling the truth.
And besides he didn't believe that he had enough blood to
take that many paternity tests. So he was history by the end
of spring; and the summer brought another clone to stand
in his place. Still another conservative, except that this one
was white.

And Abshu wondered if all of that energy had really
done any good. Was it better to have a black conservative
on the council who didn't vote with the interests of the
poor or a white one? Does it matter what color the hand
that circles your throat as you're choked to death? It was
the same result, wasn't it? Did it hurt any less because
the hand belonged to your own kind? The budgets for
libraries and arts programs were still cut to the bare bone;
Brewster Place was still slated for demolition. Some
would say that he and B.B. had been wrong in ousting
Woods. If there was one black—whatever his politics—
maybe that would make room for two some other
day. Abshu really didn't know the answers to those ques-

tions. What he knew was that he would fight Woods's successor for the programs and issues that he believed in as hard as he'd fought Woods. And he would continue to hope that somehow, in some way, his work was making a difference.

THE BARBERSHOP

If Brewster Place has something like a heartbeat, it can be found at Max's place. Max runs an old-fashioned business; he'll shave you and cut your hair, that's it; none of that unisex stuff where both men and women can go to get their hair done. It's not that women aren't welcome—even though they're not—but a woman would have no reason to come. It's real clear just by the smell of the place and look of the place that this is where men have a chance to hang out and talk. I go there about once a week myself, sometimes I'm taking a rest from the tenants, but most times it's just to chew the fat—or hear it chewed—with other men from the neighborhood.

It's nothing much. Just a small shop with four leather seats and the two barbers—Max and Henry—there to serve the customers. Those seats bear the imprint of the hundreds of men over the years. And the place has the pleasing smell of Old Spice aftershave, hair pomade, and talcum powder. The men who sit in there, reading the papers, playing checkers, or just socializing, done solved every problem in the world before the shop closes each day. And they're in there the next day to solve 'em all over again. It seems that no one's listened to them and so the world stayed in the same mess from the day before. It's a thankless job, being an armchair—or barber chair—politician. The issues they solve boil down to three subjects: white men, black men, and women. The white man carries all the guilt for messing up the world; the black man gets all the blame; and women are just a downright confusing issue that a hundred barbershop politicans wouldn't be able to solve. Why are women so difficult to get along with? "They practice," said Henry. "They practice all the time." This brings a good laugh and opinions from a half dozen others who want to top it.

"Naw, they don't practice. They're born that way."

"It's their mothers. They train 'em to be evil."

"Maybe their fathers too. I got me three girls and I tell 'em every day to watch out. There's some real dogs running around in the streets pretending to be men."

"Yeah, and all they make is babies. I told mine too, don't you bring no babies in here without showing me a husband first."

"But where she gonna find one? These young bucks today don't want no responsibility—that is, them that's left over and not stuck in jail."

"Amen to that. And it's making the white man very happy to see us caged up like animals in jail."

"The white man. The white man. I'm so sick of hearing about the white man. When are we gonna face up to our own lives and the stuff we do. The white man ain't in that bed helping these girls get pregnant just to then run off and leave 'em."

"That's exactly where they been our whole history—laying up with our women in slavery and us too scared to say anything. Look at all these colors here. Since when you see pictures of Africans that look like us. We is brown and beige and tan. Some of us pure yellow. Now where that come from but slavery and the white man's blood running in our veins.

"And our blood is running in them too. Years ago it weren't nothing for a high, high yellow black man or woman to slide on over the color line. Mixing and matching blood don't run one way, but you never hear about that."

"And you never will either. They don't wanna be reminded that there's black someplace in a lot of their families."

"Yeah, tell that to a white man, he'll haul off and die. But there's a little soot in many of them pots."

And the talk would go on like that for hours—round-robin—unless Greasy came into the shop. Whenever Greasy stumbled in, the shop would get silent as a tomb. To look at him the way he is now it's hard to imagine that this man once had a job, a home, and a future. But when crack started eating away at his brains, he lost it all in just that order: first his job as an airline ticket agent, then his brick home complete with a wife and two kids, to finally be left with a future in which his head was an empty shell, allowing only space for the winds of his nightmares to keep howling and howling. But somewhere in the back of his mind is the single thought left from his sane days that every month he must get a haircut. And so he comes in, smelling to high heaven, the seat of his pants slick as mud, and dropping the nickels and dimes that he gets from begging as he tries to count out the cost of his haircut. It's pitiful to watch him chasing the dropped coins that he can't keep in his shaking hands. And it's always the same reaction from Max. "No charge today, Greasy. Just sit on down and relax."

Max is the only barber in the place that will work on Greasy's head. It's too unpredictable when he'll start pounding on his chest and yelling, "I'm a man . . . I'm a man . . ." Any comment can set him off and so the other men have learned to just stop conversing when Greasy's in the shop. Some will even get up and leave, saying that they can't stand the stench from his unwashed body.

"You need to get off that shit and get yourself together," Max says.

"I'm trying, Max. I'm trying."

"You ain't trying hard enough," someone else will say. "And when you gonna put some water on your stinky ass?"

Greasy laughs with the rest of the men. "I'm trying, Bullet. I'm trying."

"Now don't get him going," Max says, "or I'll never finish his head."

"Max, you need business that bad you gotta work on him?"

"Every man is entitled to a shave and a haircut. For some of us, what else is left?" Max replies.

"Yeah," Greasy says, "because I'm a man—right, Max?— I'm a man . . ."

"Now look what you done, you got him started. I oughta make you work on his crazy ass. Sit still, Greasy, or I'm kicking you out of here."

But no matter how deep the pain; how tangled the threads of this man's life; Greasy's isn't the only sad story that's sat in Max's chairs. If those chairs could talk, they would be at it day and night with sadder and sadder stories. Brewster Place is a small street but it seems there's an endless supply of I coulda, I shoulda, but I didn't. Can you call it any man's blues? I don't know, but you can definitely call it the black man's blues. There's something about us and pain that keeps spinning out there in the universe to return again and again. And when you're sick and tired of being sick and tired, sometimes you get like Greasy. And if not that low or that bad, then you get like us. Hoping to solve the problems of the world so that we forget—or put the knowledge on hold—that our own lives need attention.

Yeah, if these seats could talk. They could tell you like I couldn't about Mattie's son. I knew it was Basil who spoke to me that one day in the street before he stopped by here to get his hair cut. Whenever I was up in Mattie's apartment working on a bad pipeline or doing some plastering, I saw the little shrine she kept for him. A wall of pictures from the time he was little until a grown man. Did I tell her he had come by? No. Because what could she have done with the knowledge? Say, thank you, Ben, and then go up to her apartment to grieve a little more? To me that woulda been messing with the order of things. It's not my job to bring grief to a nice woman who never had nothing but a kind word to say to me.

And then there was Eugene who came here on the day of his baby's funeral. I had spoken to him earlier in the morning and seen pain so thick I coulda cut it with a knife. You going to the funeral? he asked. No, I said, too sad with it being a baby and all. Yeah, he said, I know what you mean. I was going myself, but the way Ceil's friends look at me, damn, like I was filth or something. But I knew Eugene wasn't going to be able to take that funeral, even though he stopped by the barbershop to get a clean shave and a cut. He was grieving too hard to accept that child was dead. And I knew that his was the kind of grief that could swallow the whole world—himself included—if you let it get out of hand. I saw suicide in that boy's eyes and I prayed for him to get a grip on things. Just let the pain and the regrets wash over you; you won't drown although you'll feel like you will. No, the one fact about regrets is that they do ebb in time and you're faced with the hard decision to let your life go on or not.

Those are only two stories but these chairs have seen hundreds more. You can change the name and occupation, go up or down with their ages, and it's like it's the same man sitting there each time. What they got in common is the blues. And like they say, the blues ain't nothing but a good man crying for help. These chairs done seen many a good man as well as the bad, and the ugly. They done seen rejoicing and they done seen grief. Although a man grieves different from a woman, a whole lot more is kept inside to bite him a little here, a little there, until the blood begins to flow. And when the blood begins to flow, it'll have to fill up every space in his body before you finally see it in his eyes. Men cry as much as women—but most just cry inside.

And maybe things woulda worked out different if we had realized that was the case with Greasy—he was bleeding inside. But we were so busy being thankful that we weren't him; so busy judging and feeling superior, pitting our half a minds against his none, that we forgot he was our "brother" and where he goes we go—if we like it or not. Yeah, if we had remembered that things might have turned out real different that muggy day at the end of October.

The shop was more crowded than usual 'cause we had the weather to talk about—an Indian summer that showed no signs of letting up. And this one time I was hiding from the tenants 'cause some were gonna want me to fire up those furnaces regardless of the weather. The shop door was kept open to let in what little breeze there was and some men had stripped down to T-shirts and short pants. "It's all them rockets they sending up to the moon," said Max. "Been messing up the weather since then." Every time we had a different twist on the season—a warm winter or a cool summer—Max lay the blame on rockets being sent into outer space.

"Yeah," Henry agreed. "Things ain't been the same since them white men starting messing with the moon. Can't figure out shit to solve the problems here on earth, they gotta go take their nonsense to the moon."

"You'll never get me up there," one of the customers said.

"And me neither," joined in another.

"I didn't hear nobody asking for your monkey ass to go to the moon," Max said. "They too sick and tired of you black people right here on earth to take you someplace else. You know how that goes, let you black people move in and the neighborhood goes to the dogs."

"You black people? Since when you turned white?"

"The day I figured it might get me a shot to be an astronaut. I don't mind admitting I might like to see what's really up there."

"Turn around and look in your mirror and you'll see exactly what ain't getting up there—your black butt."

"They got black astronauts. I seen 'em in a magazine."

"Yeah, but you see any of them walking on the moon? I told you before, they don't want your monkey ass walking on the earth, so why they gonna send you to walk on the moon?"

"You see, that's what's wrong with the black man—always so negative."

"He's right about that. Before you know it, they're gonna even have black women astronauts. Wouldn't that be something?"

"Yes, Lord, that'll solve all our problems—send their nagging butts right to the moon."

As the men were laughing Greasy stepped into the shop. He had on a clean shirt and pair of pants, even though both were wrinkled. His clothes meant that he'd been picked up and taken to a shelter that he managed to escape from again and again. But at least he'd stopped smelling so bad.

"You're looking good there, Greasy," Max said. "You ain't getting married on us are you?"

"I'm trying, Max, I'm trying."

I often wondered how much Greasy understood what folks was saying to him. He had only two phrases anyone's heard him say: I'm a man. And I'm trying.

Max was still working on a customer's head so Henry, who had just finished a head, took Greasy into his chair. The house rules were if Greasy walked in he was the next customer no matter what—get him in and out fast. But this day it wasn't fast enough. For no reason—or at least I should say—for no godly reason that anyone could tell, Greasy moved toward Henry's chair, grabbed the straight razor on the counter, then grabbed Henry from behind and held the razor to his neck. Every man in there became still as a stone.

"I'm a man . . . I'm a man . . ." Greasy kept saying over and over.

"Yeah," Max said, trying to edge closer and closer to him. "You're a man . . . You're a man, Greasy, so just put down the razor."

Greasy's eyes were vacant and wild as he tightened his hold on Henry's neck. All the life had drained from Henry's face as he tried not to move an inch or even breathe too deeply. A few of the other men got up and started edging toward Greasy as well. "You're a man, Greasy," they kept say-

ing as if they were cooing to a baby—quiet and smooth—
"You're a man."

"So just put down the razor, okay?" Max said softly. "Put
it down and let Henry go. I gotta cut your hair, right? See,
it's me, Max, I always cut your hair. So put down the razor,
okay?"

"I'm trying, Max, I'm trying." And Greasy began to cry.

"That's okay," Max said, "I know you're trying. So just
put it down, okay?"

A circle of men were within three feet of him now. And
Greasy was getting confused, trying to look at them all, to
make eye contact as those wild winds howled in his head.
"I'm a man," Greasy said as he let Henry go, "I'm a man."

And then suddenly he took the straight razor and slit his
own throat. Blood from the artery in his neck gushed so
forcibly that it sprayed all along the mirrors and on every
man in the shop. And the fall that Greasy took, hitting his
head against the floor almost tore his head from his neck.

"Aw, shit," Max kept saying over and over again. "Holy
shit."

Max's place was closed for a week, and when he reopened
we had plenty to talk about. And believe it or not, it was
never about what happened to Greasy. We all remembered
what it was like to go home and wash his blood from our
clothes, our faces, and above all, our hands. To have to look
into our mirrors and lie to ourselves it wasn't our fault. We
had not made him the whipping boy for all of our troubles.
We had not held that razor to his throat and slashed. If for
all the times we had called him brother, if we had really

meant it, somehow Greasy should be alive today. But we let him down and let ourselves down as we used him for the garbage can to hold all our fears.

There's talk that Brewster Place is to be torn down. And if it's true, Max's place will be the last holdout. They better take me out in chains and handcuffs, Max is always saying, 'cause it's the only way I'm leaving here. But he'll leave, like the others leave, with the bitter taste of defeat in his mouth. Myself, I would hate to see Max's barbershop go. But it's only fitting that he would make a grandstand and fight till the end. This is the only place for us men to get together, to look into each other's eyes and see what we need to see— that we do more than just exist—we thrive and are alive.

DAWN

Brewster Place watched its last generation of children torn away from it by court orders and eviction notices, and it had become too tired and sick to help them. Those who had spawned Brewster Place, countless twilights ago, now mandated that it was to be condemned. With no heat or electricity, the water pipes froze in the winter, and arthritic cold would not leave the buildings until well into the spring. Hallways were blind holes, and plaster crumbled into snaggled gaps. Vermin bred in uncollected garbage and spread through the walls. Brewster had given what it could—all it could—to its "Afric" children, and there was just no more. So it had to watch as they packed up the remnants of their dreams and left . . .

Quiet footsteps echo on the empty street as Abshu makes his way to the stoop of the building where he grew up. An empty street feels differently, smells differently from just a quiet street. An empty street no longer breathes through the hope or despair of its tenants. It has no lingering odors from a pot of beans or a skillet of fried chicken; no lingering of perfume or aftershave. So there is no life remaining on this deserted street—but as Abshu sits down on the stoop he does hear music. He looks up at the window of the apartment where Brother Jerome used to hold sway and thinks, Someone needs to stop that child from playing. Someone needs to stop that music *now*. The battle is over; let this street go in peace. But the music plays on . . . and on . . .

And Abshu will sit through this summer night until dawn, listening to the music—and looking at the wall—and wondering for the hundredth time if there was more he could have done. More petitions. More pleading. Just more. If he had brought five hundred to City Hall instead of fifty? If he had brought a thousand . . . ten thousand? If a million men had descended on that building, would it have made a difference? Could he have saved this street? And the next one over . . . and over . . . ? He thinks not. He thinks that even with a million men they could not hold back dawn. It would take a god to do that. And with all of his effort he had not thought of praying. But he would pray now. "Our Father, who art in heaven, hallowed be thy name. Thy kingdom come. Thy will be done on earth as it is in heaven." But it was from heaven that the music came. Was it this god—or another god—who had decreed that for the sons of Brewster Place, there would always be the blues? No, he would not accept that.

Abshu clenches his hands into fists that rest on his thighs. He thinks about the power of a million men; a million voices raised to a roar to say, No, this should not be. But even the voices of a million men, a million soldiers, cannot hold back the dawn.

And so he will leave this street to walk into a rising sun. One man against the dawning of the inevitable. One man who is determined to believe that this is the end of a battle, not the end of the war. And this one tired warrior is the best that Brewster Place has to offer the world. But one man standing is all that's needed—one manchild for the millennium—as the music plays on . . . and on . . .